THE
APPOINTED
HOUR
STORIES

D0069821

SUSANNE DAVIS

Cornerstone Press
Stevens Point, WI
Est. 1984

Cornerstone Press
Department of English | University of Wisconsin-Stevens Point
2100 Main Street
Stevens Point, WI 54481

Direct inquiries to cornerstone.press@uwsp.edu
Visit our website at www.uwsp.edu/cornerstone

Library of Congress Control Number: 2017956466

ISBN 978-0-9846739-4-0

Printed in the United States of America
First Edition: December 2017

Printing, collating, and binding made possible by a generous contribution from:
Worzalla Publishing
3535 Jefferson Street
Stevens Point, WI 54481-0307

Dedication photo by David Davis.

Author photo by Tara Doyle.

Cover art by Thomas Moberg. Designed by Richard Wilkosz.

For my brother, Andrew G. Davis, Jr. (1961-2017),

a kind and gentle soul who lived and died in the woodland of eastern Connecticut, which he loved so much. May these stories in some small way honor your memory and life. I feel your spirit with me always.

TABLE OF CONTENTS

THE APPOINTED HOUR

"Let those who are sent on a journey
not permit the appointed hours to pass by...."
Chapter 50, *Rule of Saint Benedict*

PART I

The first time I was confronted with evil, I did not recognize it as evil.

I was living in Iowa when the first packet of clippings arrived with my grandmother's slanted scrawl across the envelope. Young women had started to go missing in our quiet corner of Connecticut. Our town of Asheville, with a population of two thousand people, had no traffic lights, no public transportation, only one general store, and one gas station across the street so that kids walked or peddled to the playground to smoke cigarettes away from any parents who might object.

I've been saving these, my grandmother's note read. They're all younger than you, but wasn't sure if you knew the families. You best stay in Idaho, where it's safe.

She was forever confusing Iowa with Idaho, and I attributed this to the fact that, other than crossing the border from her childhood home in Boston's east end to her marriage bed in southeastern Connecticut, my grandmother had not left the state except for one journey to

New York City to chaperone a school trip. She considered the world outside her familiar boundaries as unsafe, but now, with this news, she was not feeling secure even there.

The reports of young women disappearing from the rural backwaters of Connecticut shocked me, too. The first clipping, dated six months prior, was a missing person bulletin of sorts with a smiling photo of a fifteen-year-old girl, eyes full of innocent engagement with the photographer as she rested her chin on the head of a fluffy orange tabby cat. Her best friend had last seen the girl. The two had been at the playground after school and the missing one, Amanda Gladstone, had left for home and dinner but never arrived. This was at a time before the widespread use of cell phones.

The second clipping was dated three months later—this time a sixteen-year-old. She and a friend had been walking the rural roads of dotted stone walls and Holstein cows, smoking cigarettes and talking to boys. They had parted ways for only an hour—the teen, whose name was Cindy Lawson, walked home to put a load of laundry in for her mother and the casserole for dinner. *This is just a few miles from your old house*, my grandmother's note read.

By the time the third clipping came in the mail a month later, I had gotten busy with daily life. But when I saw my grandmother's handwriting and felt the heft of the envelope, I knew it contained more disturbing news.

I unfolded the clipping, carefully cut along the edges of the newspaper columns. My hands shook and the revulsion I felt almost kept me from reading, expecting and dreading the photograph of another young face captured by a camera during a happy moment, emphasizing the tragedy, some tragedy, to have befallen her. And it did. Not one, but two young women who had disappeared together, thirty minutes southeast of my hometown, just a few miles from my grandmother's door. Killed on Easter Sunday. *Pray for them,*

Victoria. People in our corner of the state ripped apart by this violence. I had followed my grandmother's Catholic faith, unlike others in the family, but now her words angered me. What good would prayers do?

Whereas the first two disappearances had been questioned as possible runaways, that was not so in this third instance. The young women, both fourteen, disappeared together, and their bodies were found a few days later in a culvert, faces down, arms tied behind their backs. They had been sodomized. Police believed they had a serial killer in their midst but had few clues about the killer's identity.

The next envelope came a few weeks later. The killer was on a rampage. Another young woman, seventeen, disappeared while hitchhiking. Her body was found by a jogger under a pile of rocks by the side of the road. Police called for eyewitnesses. One came forward, remembering a blue, late-model Toyota following behind the woman.

It was the breakthrough they needed. The next clipping showed the photograph of my high school classmate: Reginald Rawlins. He had been arrested and charged with the murders. Detectives had run the list of three thousand such registered cars in Connecticut. Reggie was the first one questioned, and he kept throwing out clues. Before the detective could even get out the door, Reggie had confessed to several of his killings.

My hand shook as I regarded Reggie's photo, a skinny, curly-haired twenty-four-year-old, his eyes burning with a dark intensity that I did not remember from our years together in high school. Reggie, a mass murderer?

We had both been part of the vocational agriculture program at the regional high school. Reggie had graduated from the program and gone on to study agriculture at Cornell. I left the program after two years to concentrate more fully on college prep courses and from that time on hardly ventured down the corridor that housed the ag program. But during those first two years, Reggie and I sat in classes together and worked side by side planting trees, growing vegetables for sale in the school greenhouse, and building pens to house animals on the farm land the school owned a few miles down the road. I became the editor-in-chief of the school newspaper, and when Reggie was accepted into Cornell, the paper ran a front-page story on him and his academic successes.

I scanned the clippings my grandmother had sent and then retrieved the other envelopes and slumped onto the love seat in the sunny corner of my apartment in Des Moines to read them again more carefully.

Reggie had also been arrested and charged with the murder of a young woman in New York state while he was a student at Cornell. After graduating from Cornell, he worked as an insurance agent; the authorities were still putting together the pieces, but they thought it was this job that gave him access to families' homes and their daughters, whom he then stalked, waiting for his opportunity.

I put the clippings back into the envelope and tucked the envelope on a bookshelf. I did not know what to do with what I had learned. I tried to take photographs. I was in a graduate program at the time, and I thought I could use my 35-mm camera to witness something that might somehow balance out the darkness of the events unfolding in my corner of Connecticut. I went out into the street, photographing the elm trees that lined University Avenue. But when I developed the photos, I was struck by the shadows cast by the towering limbs. What I thought I was seeing in light materialized as something ominous.

I found myself trying to remember if there had ever been any clues to Reggie's violent nature during the time I had known him. I remembered one time we were in the greenhouse together, arranging floral centerpieces to be sold at the holiday open house. I needed more potting soil, and rather than get the step stool, I asked Reggie to reach up and grab the bag off the shelf for me, which he did. He was nothing but polite. No matter how I searched or tried to look at what I had known of Reggie, I could not find any hint or inkling of a man capable of a violent act, let alone murder.

I thought a lot about evil for a while after that. I tried to understand, if in fact, evil did exist. I was going to my mailbox every day now, looking for the next missive from my grandmother. We never talked by phone. All of our communication was through the written word. And while I had a computer and the ability to research newspaper coverage daily, I waited, as though the only reliable source was my grandmother's clippings sent directly to me. Many more clippings followed as Reggie led police to the places he had buried his victims, bodies uncovered in shallow grave sites along the crumbling stone walls of eastern Connecticut, along the back roads traveled by leaf peepers and cyclists mapping century rides. These were the roads I traveled every day of my life. Nothing had screamed out to me there as foul. Could not the land speak? Could a tree not whither in protest or a stone wall collapse its guard as a way to sound the warning bell? Instead, the earth had silently accepted the mutilated bodies of these young women and held them until they could be claimed and a proper ceremony performed.

I started to sleep with the lights on in my bedroom. And I began reading a murder mystery series, frantic to uncover the criminal before the story revealed him or her. Not once could I do so. For an entire series of twenty-six murder mysteries, one for every letter in the alphabet, by the time I got to Z, I was no closer to identifying a killer than I was with A. I had just finished the series when I got news of my grandmother's cancer.

I flew home, my grandmother's most recent letter in my coat pocket. *I'm not in any pain,* she wrote. *It's not like with those girls. I've had a good long life. I am going home to be with God.*

She looked like a child huddled in her hospital bed and when I hugged her, her bones shifted like water under her skin, but her eyes radiated light and strength. I hunted down the doctor, and he reassured me she wasn't in any pain, although the tumor on her lung was the size of a baseball, making it hard for her to breathe. She didn't want chemo.

"I'm ready to go home," she said.

I wanted to ask her how she could be so sure there was anything beyond this life, but something stopped me. We passed the days talking instead about family, and I read to her from her Bible, which she had brought to the hospital with her. It was filled with prayer cards for dead relatives. One morning, I picked it up to read, and out fluttered a folded piece of notebook paper, with the names of all Reggie's victims in my grandmother's scrawl.

"Someone's got to pray for those poor girls," she said.

That afternoon while she slept, I drove out to Norwich State Hospital, where one of Reggie's victims had been found. Over its lifetime, the hospital had grown from one hundred acres to nine hundred acres. The place looked like a college campus lined with trees and clusters of brick buildings held up by white pillars. I had read from my grandmother's clippings that Reggie's mother had been committed to the hospital back when Reggie was a child, that she and Reggie's father married after she discovered she was pregnant with him. Three more children followed. Reggie's mother had hated farming and the news reported that she had beaten her children until she ran off down south with another man. Whether she had done that before or after being committed to the insane asylum, I didn't know, but Reggie had grown up without her in his life. Was he trying to say something when he brought one of his victims to the spot of his mother's incarceration? I sat, my arms braced against the steering wheel, and I hung my head out the window. As I did, I swore I heard a woman screaming. I rolled all the windows down and tried to listen more closely, but the scream, which at first sounded like it was coming from behind me, suddenly seemed to engulf me. It rocked me to the core. I rolled up the windows and sped away, back to my grandmother. She was awake when I entered her room.

"You look like you've seen a ghost," she said. "Are you all right?"

I didn't tell her I had been to one of Reggie's crime scenes, but as I picked up the Bible, I said, "Granny, why would God allow those innocent girls to die at Reggie's hands?"

"I know, honey. It's a terrible thing, isn't it?" She clasped my hands in her papery dry ones. Still, the heat felt good.

"Why would God allow it?"

She pushed herself up in the bed, her hair flat from being pressed against the pillow for so long. "It's free will— for good or bad."

"But those girls didn't have free will. Is that the best the Catholic Church can say, free will?"

"It's hard to see it from that perspective," she admitted, "but Saint Augustine says God uses everything, even suffering, to his greatest good. The Church believes God will use even this, somehow, to the service of good."

I winced.

She pulled my arm to bring me closer and dropped her voice. "That doesn't mean God isn't crying right alongside us, honey."

Thinking of God as grieving helped.

That night she fell into a semi coma and started calling the names of her dead husband, my grandfather, and relatives who had gone before her, some of their names familiar to me from the prayer cards tucked in her Bible. Her breathing became rattled and labored and during those dark hours I sang "Amazing Grace." With the morning's first light, she died. Her machine beeped, announcing her passing, and the staff came in and called the time of death, unhooked her various lines, and asked me if I wanted a few minutes alone. I nodded. They left the room and, afraid of Death surrounding me, I rushed out into the hallway and bumped into a nurse walking by. She put her hands on my shoulders to steady me, and I found myself looking into the face of a childhood friend, Katherine. We had fallen out of touch when my family moved from town, but right before that move in fourth grade, Katherine's mother, who had been my Girl Scout leader, was murdered by her stepson, Katherine's own stepbrother. I had been scared of violence since that time.

"Victoria? What are you doing here?" she asked.

"My grandmother. She just died." I pointed into the room.

Katherine took me by the elbow, and we went back into the room.

"She looks peaceful now, doesn't she?" she asked. She went over to the bed and beckoned me to stand beside her. She tucked the sheet up around my grandmother's shoulders, and I felt the tears coming. "Can I ask you something, Katherine?" I didn't even know myself what I was going to ask.

The room, dimly lit, caught the light in her blue eyes. It was the same light my grandmother's eyes had shone.

"How did you get through it? What your stepbrother did to your mother?"

I was afraid she would recoil from me at such a blunt question, but instead she put an arm over my shoulder and gave me a hug. Her eyes went to the nightstand and my grandmother's Bible.

"I didn't get through it alone. My aunt was the one to tell me what happened to my mother and as she was telling me I felt—I don't know—that somehow I was not going to be alone."

Her beeper went off then. "I have to get back to my patients," she said. She scribbled her number on a slip of paper. "Call me if you want, Victoria, okay?"

I shoved the paper in my pocket, and Katherine took my hand and put it on my grandmother's hand before she left the room.

After the funeral, I took a week to clean out my grand-mother's apartment. She had a statue of Mary about three feet tall, with blue robes that draped around her and fell with a gentle fold, revealing the white of a dove's belly. Her hands, clasped in prayer, held my grandmother's rosary beads. I set her on the kitchen table in a cardboard box with the last things to go to Goodwill. As I walked back and forth, closing windows and sweeping dust bunnies from corners, I felt she was watching me. I locked the door for the last time, carried the box to the car, and drove to Goodwill, where I handed her over to one of the attendants. But as he carried her toward the bin, I reached out and plucked her back, set her in the front seat beside me and drove off. Back in Iowa, Mary stayed in the corner of my bedroom. Before long, I was able to sleep with the lights off.

Shortly after my grandmother's death, I moved back to Connecticut. Reggie was given the death sentence, the first person sentenced to death row in Connecticut in forty years. There were protests, delays, and appeals. Reggie's case dragged on for twenty years, but ultimately, the court's ruling was upheld, and on May 13, 2005, Reggie Rawlins received death by lethal injection.

The end did not come soon enough. During those twenty years it took for the specter of Reggie Rawlins to pass from this world, there could be little peace for families called to court over and over again. I want to say I thought about Reggie very little, but it's not true. I wished that I had my grandmother to help me understand the things I didn't understand. After his death, little by little, memory of him faded.

PART II

But Reggie getting the death penalty didn't make me less afraid. The fear ran like a weak current under my skin for almost a decade until I had to confront it again. I was teaching creative writing at the state university, just thirty minutes from where Reggie was executed, to an advanced class comprised of students I had taught before.

The semester had gone well, I thought. We had just two more meetings. One of the last remaining poets was to submit work for comment and workshopping. I printed the poems and began reading. He prefaced the work by acknowledging that it was disturbing. In truth, it was more than disturbing. It was filled with hate in the form of racial and sexual slurs of the highest charge. Dark language gave voice to dark thoughts, too dark to reprint or repeat. How had I missed this inclination in his previous writing?

Half the class did not show up for workshopping. One student emailed to tell me that there had been an incident in the classroom with the same student a month earlier, when I had been conducting conferences in my office. The students had been sharing work with each other in the classroom and apparently, this student had shared material the other students considered homophobic and downright scary.

No one had told me.

This experience sent me to thinking about Reggie. The student's poem was filled with hate, but was it the same level of violence as the morally reprehensible act of a serial killer? No. He had not acted on his beliefs, but really, did I even know that? Did freedom of speech laws protect this student's individual rights to express such views, even if it was clear the content wasn't appropriate for a classroom? Something about the destructive charge of the language harkened back to the loss of innocence I experienced when Reggie murdered the young women. And I wondered if my own naiveté had allowed this misguided student a platform for his destructive writing.

I rummaged around that evening for my grandmother's Bible and found it in the closet, with the statue of Mary; she had been relegated there too. Folded inside the Bible was one of the newspaper stories about Reggie. A young girl had written a letter to Reggie and gotten a response from him, which the local newspaper had published. He had written that he had a condition of sexual dysfunction that was being helped by medication, and horrible though his actions were, he had been forgiven when he accepted Christ into his life. Reggie claimed his uncle, who committed suicide when Reggie was six years old, had sexually abused him. The paper reported the courtroom testimony that Reggie had exhibited antisocial behavior at a young age and had been sexually inappropriate with young girls in his neighborhood as a child. My grandmother had never shared this clipping with me. I had not seen or known this part of Reggie's story.

Could there have been healing for Reggie? When he was in prison, he took medications that tempered his destructive sexual urges. The article went on to report that Reggie became a devout Catholic in prison. He became an oblate to a Benedictine monastery in Connecticut, and it was at this monastery that his remains were buried. I tried to imagine Reggie on death row praying the set form of prayers and psalms and Bible readings. There had been intervention in the early stages of his sexual violence. He had been caught molesting a teenager; he had been arrested, incarcerated, evaluated, and paroled. The law had suggested he take up a passtime, like jogging, to divert his sexual attention. I felt angry at the authorities even though they later admitted to a grave misunderstanding of the brewing danger within Reggie. He had been released and his release freed him to begin his killing rampage.

That night, I had a dream I was back at the hospital with Katherine, standing over my grandmother's body, and she was saying over and over, "I was never alone." In my dream I was thinking, *Why does she keep repeating that? Doesn't she know I heard her the first time?*

I woke up with the light beating down on me and Mary staring me in the face.

I got up, turned on my computer, and began composing an email to my department head. She emailed back a few hours later, suggesting I contact an on-campus office designed to give support in such situations. There were institutional supports. Columbine and Newtown and Virginia Tech and too many others to name were starting to help us understand the power of intervention to avert disaster. I put aside my anger over the fact my students had mostly been so silent. I understood their fear. We had all seen and feared too much. Was it part of evil's nature to take innocence and paralyze people with fear?

I was not sure how it would all turn out. Would there be help for the student? An opportunity for psychological therapy and healing, if needed? And how was one to know if it was warranted? I found myself looking for any clues I might have missed. A few came to mind. They were subtle, but they were there, and I chastised myself. Although I did not feel comfortable equating my student's hate poem with Reggie's acts of sexual sadism, Katherine's words "I was never alone" reverberated through me as I printed out the Morning Prayer for the Daily Hours.

"O God, come to our assistance. O Lord, make haste to help us." The ancient Benedictine prayer could not erase the violence done by Reggie, but could its three thousand years of practice have power to shine more light in the world? I chose to believe so. Then I picked up the phone, dialed the university office the department head had given me, and asked to speak to the person in charge of community standards.

THE OBJECT OF DESIRE

After my mother died, I was left alone on our rundown farm with the wind moaning through the cracks, doors slamming in empty rooms, bills piling up on the kitchen table, and nightmares of Troy. The nightmares had faded for a while but now resurfaced, making sleep so difficult I finally went to my doctor for some sleeping pills. She started asking one question after another until finally, like a bloodhound, she had flushed out what she called "the root of my problem." She promised me some narcotic help only if I signed up for therapy.

Starting in April, every Wednesday night I drove to a little clapboard house in a neighborhood near Belaport's hospital and sat in a cozy living room. That's where I heard the stories of Cleo, who was raped by her drug-addicted boyfriend, and of Donna, who was a college freshman when a guy followed her home from her first night at a bar and raped her while she was passed out on her bunk. An armed intruder raped Dolores, a sixty-five-year-old widow, in her bed. Missy was barely thirteen when her minister's son raped her.

During our ninety-minute sessions, I said only four words: "Andrea. And I pass." I was under no obligation to say anything more than my name. I kept listening for the part of each story that told how the women were to blame, which, in my heart, I believed to be true, followed by the judgment of the group. Again, I believed we all deserved that, but I could not detect where to blame any of them, while Mona King, our group facilitator, kept reassuring each woman that she was *not* to blame.

I began to look forward to the sessions, even though I didn't speak much. One night on my way there, I picked up my mail and found a certified letter. When I saw the envelope's green sticker, I decided it was from Troy, even though he and I were divorced and the return address was a local law firm. I stuffed the letter in my purse, unopened.

That night was the fourth week at group, and everyone but me had shared her story. The women were quiet, and Mona, trying hard to reach us, told us about her own rape. Still, none of us spoke. As if proving that exact point, she pulled her blazer tight around her petite frame and sent around the circle a bucket of affirmations, asking us each to take one. When we were all holding a piece of folded paper, she turned to me.

"Andrea, will you please read yours to the group?"

I took a deep breath. "'Never doubt that a small group of thoughtful and committed individuals can change the world. Indeed, it is the only thing that ever has.'"

Mona looked around the circle. "I want each of you to take these home and reflect on them."

I crumpled up my paper.

Mona turned back to me. "Andrea, why did you do that?"

She was staring me straight in the eye. I noticed how her nails were perfectly painted and the color matched her lipstick and everything about her looked cared for.

"Because it's shit," I said. "And don't try to bond with me, Mona. Like you know exactly how we feel!"

Mona drew in her breath.

"Not one of us controlled what happened to us, so who are we kidding about changing the world?"

If Mona had said one word in response, if any of those women had said one word, I was going to walk out, but there was total silence in that room. I had spoken more than I had in a month and the silence was like water freezing between my story and me.

"For a month, I've been listening to you all blame yourselves. Donna, you saying, 'Oh, if I hadn't drank so much,' and you, Cleo, 'If I hadn't let him in the apartment when he was high,' and Dolores, 'I should have locked my door.' And Missy, 'Oh, I should have told my parents.' Mona, you keep saying it's not our fault. Shift the blame away from the victim. Back to the perpetrator. But—" I felt the muscles constrict in my throat.

I gulped and gasped and jumped up to peer out the window. Then I was pacing back and forth, gripping my hands to keep them from shaking.

"You want to talk stupid? You want to talk blame? I met Troy at an A.A. meeting in Atlanta. I was living with my aunt, trying to get away from my mother. My aunt didn't like Troy, and he didn't like her. First alarm. So what do I do? Move in with him. He takes me to the Sky Top strip club and his friends say, 'She's so beautiful Troy. Let her go up there, man. She should be dancing.' Troy says no. That's good, right? But meanwhile, we're three months behind on rent, the truck needs brakes, blah blah blah. So I push, 'The girls seem happy, Troy. They've got makeup and clothes and gym passes.' I say, 'We can use this money. Get married. Start a family.' That's what Troy wanted, a family. The deal was six months. A year goes by. We pay the bills, get married, and move into a bigger apartment. I say, 'Okay, Troy, time for a baby.' He says, 'Just three more months, to get some savings.' I don't want to, but it's just three months, so I do it.

"Then one night, three college boys came in. They were loud and obnoxious, and they left me a hundred dollar bill with their phone numbers on it. When my shift was over, I went out back to get in Troy's truck. He was drinking. He hadn't had a drink since I met him. He asked for my money, and I gave it to him and when he saw the phone numbers, he hit me. 'Whore.' That's all he said. Like I wasn't even good enough for more than one word. He started driving crazy, and I told him, 'You're the one who didn't want me to stop, Troy. You're scaring me.' I tried to jump out, but he grabbed me by the throat and held me that way, drinking and driving with one hand until we got to the truck stop where all his buddies were holed up for the night, playing cards and drinking whiskey. I jumped out of the cab. My knees got all scraped up. He caught me and—"

Only I couldn't say it. Not even to them. "Three of them." I held up my fingers. My voice faltered. "Because he said if he hadn't been there, that's what I would have done with those college boys."

"Andrea," Mona said. "This is not your fault."

"Well, whose fucking fault is it?" I screamed. "I was a fucking stripper."

"Your husband's," she answered evenly. "The other men's. Not yours."

That's when I let go and cried, because for a month, I had listened to her say those words to the other women.

"You didn't deserve to be raped, Andrea. None of you did. You deserve better and when you see that, you're going to get angry." Mona nodded. "When you get angry, that little piece of paper is going to start to mean something to you."

Mona's words were like a promise—one I didn't believe but wanted to. Only our elder, Dolores, went to the police after her rape. The rest of us had all been too afraid—afraid no one would believe us, afraid it was our fault, afraid we got what we deserved.

"Let's find Andrea's husband and kill him," Cleo suggested, for they all agreed that my story was the most horrific, even though Mona tried to stop them from saying so.

"That's disassociating from your own painful experiences," she said, pulling her blazer tighter around herself.

"*Dis* this," said Cleo, flipping her the finger.

"What's that? I can't hear you," Dolores, our senior, yelled.

"I've heard this so many times, I'm numb," Donna mumbled.

"You mean *dumb*," Missy shot across the room.

We all laughed.

A few days later, I had just put on a relaxation tape when I heard a knock on the door. It was a middle-aged man in a tweed jacket and wire-rim glasses. He knocked one, two, three more times. My heart pounded, my throat closed, sweat sprouted, muscles contracted, and I stayed hidden behind the lounge chair. I thought about the unopened letter in my purse and this guy knocking at my door at ten a.m. Troy must have sent him to kill me for talking. My mother had told Troy the one time he'd called that if he ever contacted me again, we'd report him. We got an unlisted number, and I hadn't heard from him since, but I was convinced this stranger in tweed was connected to Troy. After he drove away in a Lincoln Town Car, I checked the doors and windows and walked around holding my cell phone.

A working phone had become a powerful necessity after my relationship with Troy. One day shortly after we were married, one of the other dancers invited me to go see a movie with her. Troy was to be away hauling, so I said, "Yes, I'd love to." When I got off the phone, Troy was standing behind me.

"Why don't you call her back and change it to a night I can go?" he asked.

"This will give me something to do while you're gone."

Troy frowned. "Why do you need something to do?"

I didn't answer at first, and then I said, "Troy, it's just a movie. With Sheila."

Troy picked up the phone and held it out to me.

"What should I say? This is stupid, Troy." But his face flushed red and he gripped the phone tight, pulling on the cord. I called Sheila and told her some lie about having forgotten a prior commitment.

When I hung up, Troy put his arms around me. "I can't have my beautiful wife going out alone at night if I'm not there to protect her." He started whispering sweet things in my ear and we ended up in bed. The next day, Troy got us an unlisted number and wouldn't let me give it out to anyone. "This is only while you have this job. You just never know about these guys."

The next week in group, we talked about our triggers, the things that made us relive our rape, and how we handled those triggers. Donna had taken up running. Missy, who had endured three years of repeated rape and psychological battering from the minister's son, worked in an animal shelter for abused and abandoned pets. Dolores loved to cook. Cleo was a big self-talker, giving herself positive messages all day long. At night, she took up knitting.

Mona turned to me. "How about you, Andrea? What's your trigger?"

I shrugged.

She smiled. "Can't you think of anything?"

"I don't like to be pushed," I said.

Mona leaned forward, folding her hands together. "Okay, we'll go with that. You don't like to be pushed. Do you mean physically? Emotionally?" She opened her hands, appealing to me.

"I don't like to be pushed any way at all."

Mona tightened her lips, but before she could decide how or if she should respond to me, there was a disgusted sigh from the corner.

"You think you're above us, don't you?" Cleo's face was severe. Her eyes flashed hard on me. "What's the matter? You afraid of me? Or you just afraid of the truth?"

"Cleo!" Mona stood up, but I jumped in front of her.

"The truth is, I'm afraid of everything. Okay, Miss Volcano Eruption? Is that okay with you?" I don't know where those silly words came from, but that's what came out and I was standing over Cleo waiting for a fight when, all of a sudden, her face smoothed out and out came a whoop like I never heard, followed by another, then her shoulders shook, and it was clear she was laughing. Suddenly, I was laughing too, then all the women were laughing, and Mona was standing, a little uneasy, all by herself. She glanced at her watch and dismissed us for the week, asking me to think about what set me off and what constructive things I could do to pacify myself.

I tried to think about how to calm myself. But the truth was, even though the rape had happened nearly a year ago, I hadn't found ways to help myself. My mother had nursed me through the initial trauma, singing my childhood lullaby to me, drawing me warm baths, cooking all my comfort foods including chicken and biscuits, my favorite. While it was true she hadn't shown much maternal instinct earlier in my life, she certainly poured it on after I showed up on her doorstep, not having seen her for nearly four years. Then, as if the strain of it was too much for her, she suffered a massive heart attack while at the ATM. Now that she was dead, I was lost again, having gone from relying totally on Troy to relying totally on her.

That week, I went grocery shopping and bought the ingredients for chicken and biscuits. Then I went to the customer service counter to pay my electric bill. When I pulled out my wallet, the certified letter fluttered out, and the clerk picked it up and handed it back. I stuffed it deep into my purse. The letter was like a shadow darting around a corner, not there at all if I didn't pay attention to it. I went home and cooked the chicken and biscuits, forgetting the pan in the oven until I smelled burning.

The women in the group knew that I lived on a farm, the only farm left in the city proper. The next week, they brought me a shovel, rake, and hoe, and some bulbs to plant. It had been Cleo's idea. When I protested that I couldn't take the gift, Cleo said, "Just shut up and plant me some lilies. My birthday's in June, and nobody's ever brought me flowers. I'd like some damned lilies. Is that a direct enough request, Mona?"

Mona had been coaching us on how to ask for what we needed. "That's a very good job, Cleo." Mona loved Cleo, foul language and all, because she tried harder than all of us put together.

The following morning, I was just putting on a pair of overalls and a straw hat when I heard a knock at the door. It was the man in the suit, again. I hid behind the dining room door. This time, after he left, I checked the windows, doors, and phone and also pulled the shades. The sun of the bright day leaked in anyway, making me feel like a failure.

I scrubbed the counter, straightened the mail, cleaned the refrigerator, scoured the bathroom with bleach, but I could not get myself to open the door and go outside. Each time I tried, my legs went weak and my heart pounded. I don't know how much time went by, but finally I found myself with the unopened envelope in my hand. I was angry and afraid. The letter weighed nothing. It was just a letter. It couldn't hurt me. I stuffed it into the pocket of my overalls and yanked open the door, armed with the gardening tools the women had brought me.

The sun slanted away from me, and I dug for hours, pouring all my fear into the task of breaking up the hard earth, chopping the clods into a fine mix, tossing loose stones atop the old stone wall bordering the yard. When I was finished, I felt high, a better high than with the drugs I used to take when

I was dancing. But the garden needed something more, and before I knew it, I was back in the house, climbing into the attic.

I remembered seeing a show on TV where some fancy gardener potted plants in broken wicker chairs. After my mother died, I had sold some of the old furniture. Now my gaze caught the old wardrobe that stood at the one long window looking out to the fields. I went and opened it, releasing the dry pine scent and all its secrets. There hung the dress that as a child I pretended I was getting married in, the silk so aged and stiff it felt like linen. I stripped out of my clothes and stepped into it, expecting the sleeves to flop over as they had when I was a kid, but the dress fit perfectly. I smoothed the bodice and tied the satin ribbon.

When Troy and I got married in the Justice of the Peace office, I wore a gauzy white blouse with silver buttons and he wore blue jeans, and we followed the ceremony with an afternoon of sex before I went back to work dancing for other men. We had dreamed of children and a large house filled with their screeching laughter.

Suddenly, I smelled the diesel of Troy's truck and felt his deadly strength pressing against my throat. I started to gag. I was sure I heard footsteps behind me, so I stepped into the wardrobe and crouched down. There were the men again, standing in the shadow, then on top of me, one at a time. I squeezed my eyes shut and when I opened them, I was on the ceiling looking down, wondering how that woman's knees got cut and bruised when no one was touching her. And even though I was on the ceiling, I felt afraid to look into her eyes. I wondered, *Who is crying? Who is that?* I put my hands out, feeling the walls of the wardrobe, trying to talk myself back to reality, and that's when I felt the packet of letters, shoved in the back corner. I poked my head out of the wardrobe, into the daylight, and stepped out with the letters.

I untied the satin ribbon fastening them together. The first letter was dated October 1857, in bold and awkward handwriting, from someone named Elias addressed to Mary Louise. He told the story of his grandmother, Sarah Carpenter, who had borne ten children and was deserted by her husband and left to raise them on her own and work the farm as well. He mentioned that they had erected a monument to her. I remembered seeing it on a high knoll in back, although I had never heard the story about it. The letter went on:

So, Mary Louise, the will of the Brewster family owes itself to this woman, my grandmother. But our ties to this land go back even further, for I am a direct descendent of Major John Mason, the first major in Connecticut and a long-time lieutenant governor. He was the founder of Belaport, having received from the Mohegan chief, Uncas, nine square miles of land, blessed with many riches: rivers and harbor, and on its outskirts, fertile farmland, where our farm now lies. The Mohegans wrested this land from the Pequots, who were the first children of the soil and the unfortunate victims of both English and tribal aggression. That was nearly two hundred and fifty years ago, but there are times when I am laboring in the fields that I swear I see an Indian leap across my path. These visions both thrill and terrify me. For the land holds sway over me, it is my soul. This I must say: in that I am a man who feels deeply, you would find satisfaction. Marry me and we will make a family to prosper on this land. Choose me and this land for all eternity. I await your reply, Elias.

The second letter was postmarked two months later from Nebraska.

Dear Elias, Your letters are such poetry. Your sentiments, your dreams inspire me. You ask me to marry you, to choose you. Yes, dear Elias. Already, I see you and your vision of the land as you describe it. As a child, I desired adventure and a life away from here. I promise that the dream of the land will be my dream as well and the dream I will help cultivate in the children from our union, God willing in this, as in all things.

When I got done reading those letters, my head full of romantic images, I felt calm. I looked up and caught my gaze in a standing mirror along the opposite wall. The sunlight slanted through the window and shone on my dark hair, lighting up half my face and leaving the other half in shadow. Outside, my little garden plot looked like an embryo carved into the otherwise barren land.

That next week at group, I reported how good it felt to take care of something, to be in control over where a certain flower would bloom, where a life would shine forth. I told them about finding the letters in the attic and how my ancestors felt about the land, and wasn't it a coincidence that just as I was planting a garden, I should find something that had been there almost one hundred fifty years?

Mona smiled the whole time. What I described sounded so good, the women organized a group gardening day. All of us except Mona, who needed to "maintain her boundaries," met at my house on the following Saturday. We had so much fun, we decided to meet every week. The dirt flew during those gardening sessions and, when we were done planting and pruning, we put on our walking shoes and went walking through the fallow fields following the crumbling stone walls.

One beautiful morning in June, dressed in my overalls and waiting for the women to arrive, I felt ready to read the certified letter. Life seemed so different in those few short weeks, I felt sure I could handle its contents. I ripped it open, scanning the type quickly.

It wasn't from Troy at all. Some corporation called AXZ, representing the Mohegan Indian Tribe, wanted to buy my two hundred acres for five hundred thousand dollars. Relief flooded through me, mixed with a new fear. Should I sell the very land that was giving me and the other women such a sense of renewal? When the women pulled up, I stuffed the letter in my pocket, feeling sick in the stomach as they exclaimed over the irises and day lilies that had sprung up.

Cleo suggested we celebrate by taking a picnic lunch into the woods.

"But what are you going to feed us?" she demanded, flipping through the cupboards of Mason jars covered with dust. "Not this shit." Before I could reply, she was out the door picking sage from the herb garden we had planted. She came back into the kitchen, and offered the leaves to Dolores. "Okay, chef, do your magic." Dolores started chopping and sautéing, clucking over my use of corn oil. While she was filling the kitchen with delicious smells, Missy fed the cats bowls of milk. I stood staring out the window until Cleo tugged on my arm, holding a basket of golden biscuits and a thermos of mint tea, demanding me to lead the way.

We crossed the fields to the cemetery high on a hill, surrounded by overgrowth. We stepped over the broken wrought iron fence and cleared some branches before we sat and spread out our feast. Fields surrounded us on all sides. Leaves rustled lullabies. We were quiet, munching biscuits and drinking tea. Just miles away two casinos spread over hundreds of acres as the Pequots and Mohegans battled again, only this time over money. I tried to imagine the Mohegans' expansion on this hill with roads leading up to it, crisscrossing the land. It looked and felt like rape.

Cleo broke the silence. "What do you guys think you'd be doing now if you never got raped?"

Mona had encouraged us to explore how "the violence done to us had interrupted our deepest desires." She was always turning our shit into poetry like that, which was annoying, but she said it made us less likely to stuff it all away.

Donna started reading the markers. "Look, this baby was just five days old. Listen to this. 'God gave. He took. He will restore. He doeth all things well.' How depressing," she said.

"That's avoidance, honey." Cleo enjoyed playing Mona with us.

Donna picked up a twig and started breaking it to pieces. "Alright, then. I'd be an investment manager instead of a bank teller."

I was thinking about the letters I had found, so full of hope and desire, so full of their own destiny, and children to create that destiny. These women had become my family. What would happen to that family if I sold the land?

Suddenly, Cleo was shouting at me, "Earth to Andrea. I said, I'd still be doing drugs. So does that make me better off now?" She grinned and showed the chipped tooth that resulted from fighting her ex-boyfriend.

"I guess," I said.

"Come on. Why do you always hang back like that?"

"Leave her alone, Cleo," Missy said. "She's not one of your stray animals. She's a big girl. Aren't you, Andrea?"

"Yep." I was squinting at the monument that rose over my head. The long list of children's names seemed to go on forever.

"So? Maybe you'd still be dancing then?"

I hit Cleo so fast she rolled like a potato, but then she recovered and twisted, and I was on the bottom. I kneed her in the groin, and when she hunched forward I threw her over and knelt on her chest. My fist connected with her cheek, then it grazed off the bone and hit a rock. Donna and Dolores were trying to pull me off, but Cleo was lying there, kicking her feet and crying, but not fighting back. That's what stopped me: seeing her, leaves in her kinky black hair, tears glistening on her cheeks, leaking through her hands.

I knelt down and hugged her. "I'm sorry, Cleo. I'm so sorry."

She shook her head and rolled away from me, curling her knees to her chest.

"Cleo," I whispered. "Cleo, please forgive me." I was kneeling over her, sobbing the words under my breath, but they carried on the open air. She smelled like fresh air and sage, nothing hidden or rotten about her. "Cleo, I'd have a dozen kids. That's what I'd be doing. Like my ancestor." I pointed to the monument. "But I can't, Cleo. That's what the gynecologist said. Because of the rape."

Cleo rolled over and sat up. She wiped her face with her sleeve. "Those fuckers," she hissed. She hugged me, but it was like she had punched a hole in my lung. I felt so deflated. I tried to breathe but couldn't. I picked up the picnic basket and the others gathered the thermos and papers and followed along behind as I led the way back to the house. I caught sight of taillights pulling out of the driveway, but the driver didn't see us, and I was glad. When we got to the house, the women silently gathered their belongings and left the picnic remnants on the porch.

"See you at group?" Missy asked.

I darted a glance at Cleo, but she was looking back toward the knoll, one hand raised to the welt on her cheek. She turned then, and her face looked like a gaping hole where the spirit had blown out. The sight of her broke my heart.

"We didn't deserve it, Cleo," I said fervently. "None of us did."

I was so angry, looking around at the circle of faces I had come to love, faces so vulnerable, so hurt, and still so damned beautiful. It seemed to me that we had just gone backward in a very short time, but then I decided that maybe for the first time I was truly seeing the wrong that had been done to us. Cleo spun away and got in her car before I could find words to speak. The others followed.

When I carried the picnic remains into the house, I was struck by its emptiness. Just an hour earlier, the kitchen had been filled with women talking and laughing, kittens rubbing against our legs, and the smell of herbs cooking. I stood facing the refrigerator and stared at the saying hanging between two magnets from the crisis hotline: "… a small group… committed individuals… can change the world…." I felt a cold rage chill my bones. Mona was right. None of us had deserved it.

That night, I had nightmares like I hadn't had for months. Troy lurking in the basement, then outside, with his face pressed to the door, beckoning me to open it. And, for some reason, I did—only, when I opened the door, he was gone. I woke up and got out of bed to watch the sun rise. Then, I showered and went out to cut some flowers, lilies for Cleo and irises for the others. I knew where they all lived although I had never been to their homes. Cleo was sharing an apartment with her sister and three nieces and nephews. One of the children opened the door and regarded me warily. I recognized the look. Cleo came out into the hallway. I handed her the lilies.

"My birthday's not 'til the twenty-seventh," she said, folding her arms across her chest.

"Who says you can't get flowers twice?"

She grinned and took the flowers, and that's when I laid out my plan. As I talked, her grin widened. When I had finished talking she said, "They can't take our land." Then she went back in to put her flowers in water before accompanying me to visit the others.

It is amazing how much can be accomplished by a few people working together. By Sunday, we had cleaned and painted the upstairs bedrooms and put a bed, bureau, and nightstand in every room. We ripped the old linoleum off the kitchen floor, because Dolores said she couldn't cook in a kitchen like that. She wasn't going to move in with us, since she had her own house, but she wanted to test out our community as a possible bed and breakfast.

We all had plans, and we spent the weekend dreaming and talking big as we worked. We took a break each day for our walk through the fields, although we stayed away from the knoll. Without saying it, I think we all still felt too close to our ghosts. We planned what we would say when we called Mona with our news on Monday, what we would feed her for dinner when she came to visit, and which flowers might be blooming by then. We were making so much noise I almost didn't hear the knock on the door. Cleo and Donna were upstairs gathering screens to be repaired, Dolores was making lunch, and Missy was in the basement folding laundry—just like a real family. Through the window I saw the guy in the tweed jacket, waiting at the door.

I called to the women. As they gathered behind me, I thought Elias and Mary Louise would be proud of our commitment, even if we were an odd kind of family. I rehearsed how I would say, politely, we didn't intend to sell this land for gambling and slot machines, not for anything.

Then I went and opened the door.

Dancing at the Sky Top with Andrea

My code name is Andrea, emphasis on "dre" like "dream" because that's the way I move: I pretend I'm in a dream and the end of the runway blurs into a fog so thick I don't see the men in front of me. When I call my mother and tell her, "Mom, I'm working as an exotic dancer," I try to soften the blow by adding, "This is helping me take care of myself. I have to now, because I'm selling my looks." I've had problems eating in the past, but I'm over them, thanks to A.A. and Troy Germaine, my fiancé. We met at an A.A. meeting.

I call Troy my southern gentleman, but he says he's not because he lived in New Jersey and Pennsylvania when his mother was married to his father. They broke up when Troy was eight, and this still disturbs him deeply. Whenever we pass the playground in our neighborhood where a man plays basketball with his son on Saturdays, Troy stops to watch. The little boy, who's six or seven, dribbles the ball to the basket, and his father lifts him so he can dunk it. Every time they do this, they roar and hoot like Olympic stars. Troy's comment each time is as predictable as their play. "Man, I can't wait to be a daddy," he says.

We both agree we need to get our feet on the ground first. I've had issues with eating and Troy has issues too—mainly, his drinking. The first night I heard Troy speak at A.A., he said in a southern accent, "My name is Troy. I've done some things I'm not proud to admit. And I'm an alcoholic." He looked straight at me and ran his hand over his thick brown hair, cut so it showed the beautiful shape of his face. His wide-set eyes were the gray color of stormy waters, and his full lips were just right for kissing. I fell in love. Later, over coffee, Troy told me he'd been sober for six months but every day he still craved liquor and was learning to live with that desire.

Troy takes me to the Sky Top on our third date. I feel the electricity way out in the parking lot; the neon lights of the club pull us in like fish caught in a current. Guys slap Troy on the back, offer to buy us drinks. I worry he might drink, but Troy orders tonic water and so do I. Heads turn for us, for Troy I think, since everybody seems to know and like him but then I realize they're staring at me. Because at the Sky Top, life is all about the girls—beautiful, sexy, and out of reach. The stage runs across the front of the room and juts out in the center where the girls strut, kick, shake, and twirl, all hair and limbs and naked skin. Each girl is like a flashing jewel in the hot lights, surrounded by the sound of pounding music and the men who come to watch.

After a few visits to the Sky Top, where Troy's friends say, "Troy, she should be up there, man. She's prettier than all of them," I start thinking about it—men admiring me, paying money just to look at me, a lot of money… and what that money could buy. One day, I come home with my own thigh-high boots and dancer's license.

"No way," Troy says. He picks up our little kitten, Skunk, who we found outside eating garbage, and squeezes him tight to his chest. "No way." We live in a one-room apartment, and he paces back and forth between the kitchen sink and the bed.

"We got something real here," he says, running his thumb back and forth over his lips. "I don't want you working at that club."

"Why not?" I ask. "You take me there socially. Why can't I work there? I'd just go and do my job and come home, Troy. To you."

"For how long?" Troy squeezes Skunk again, and the kitten meows and jumps from his arms. We both watch him scramble out of reach. "Maybe all those guys would be too tempting. I want to be with you forever, and I don't want either of us to do anything to mess it up."

I argue, "We could make it work. I'd make at least five hundred dollars a week, enough money to get a bigger apartment and my cosmetology license. Then we'd be set up to start a family."

Troy cocks his head. "You'd feel ready then? To start a family?"

"If we could have these other things, yes."

Troy takes the boots out of my hand, and his gray eyes search mine. "Twenty-six thousand dollars is a lot of money," he says. "How about if we agree that you dance for just a year?"

So I agree, and that's how I get started dancing.

Our club manager, Marilyn, gave up dancing to have her family. Now, she works nights when her husband can be home with the kids. She's my inspiration. After all day with her kids, she comes in and plays mother to us. She arranged for discounted memberships at the Y, personal lockers, and even got the club to pay half for classes on health and makeup application. Everybody says the Sky Top girls are the most beautiful girls in the city. And it's thanks to Marilyn.

Everything goes smooth the first few months, and then one day Marilyn leaves a note for me to see her. I go to her office and knock. Marilyn—she's a tall, big-boned woman with silver blond hair—gets up from her desk, pulls me into the room, and closes the door. The room is enormous, with a white leather couch that covers two walls and a lemon tree in a white ceramic pot and a floral pastel carpet. She slides her red, cat-eye glasses off her nose and gives me that look of motherly concern.

"Hon, have you been losing weight? You don't look good."

"I know. I've got a lot of stress right now." I blurt out that Troy and I want to get married, but we need more money to get our feet on the ground. I tell her how Troy got caught driving with a suspended license, which was suspended for driving under the influence, and now he's got a probationary fine to pay to boot. We haven't been able to keep up on all our bills, so his payments lapsed, and they slapped him with a penalty and a warrant for his arrest. We have to pay the fine, the penalty, and get the warrant revoked before we can get married.

I probably wouldn't tell Marilyn any of this normally, but the night before I called my mother and asked to borrow the two hundred dollars from her.

"Right, Andrea. You think I have that kind of money? You have no sense of reality, do you?"

That's my mother. She's been living on welfare since my father died ten years ago and when she needs money she begs, lies, manipulates, but she doesn't work for it. She made sure to keep me home so she could get my Social Security every month, but as soon as I turned eighteen and the payments stopped, she wanted my entire paycheck from the A&P. I refused, so she kicked me out. When I talk to my friends back at the store, they tell me she brings in expired coupons and demands double discounts. Out of respect for me, they do it, giving her credit toward things like powdered donuts, tater tots, and nose spray. On the phone, I tell her I'm glad I escaped when I did.

"Oh yeah, Andrea. You're full of bitterness. And you think you're ready for marriage?"

Marilyn, on the other hand, listens. "Andrea, honey, you promise not to lose any more weight and I'll help you find a solution."

A few days later, she summons me again, this time motioning me to the leather couch. I squirm, trying to adjust my hip hugger shorts, red bandanna bra, and leather holster. It's hard to keep things covered sitting down. These guys don't like skin and bone. Marilyn has said more than once they want to dream about holding on to something, but under these bright lights it looks like bumps and ripples—fat—to me.

Marilyn, knowing my history, turns off the overhead light and sits next to me. "You will be surprised when I tell you this, Andrea, because I know you try not to notice, but there's a very prominent business man who comes in here sometimes on Friday afternoons. He's been a friend of mine for many years. We grew up together in the suburbs. A very fine man. His wife died, oh, three years ago now. That's when he started coming in. He just wanted to be around women—not date or anything—and it's hard to do that as you get older." Marilyn holds my gaze until she seems satisfied of something. "Anyway, when he saw you he told me, 'My God, it's Eileen.' He thinks you look just like his wife."

"Was she pretty?" I ask.

Marilyn nods. "She was a beauty. Not quite as beautiful as you, but the same exotic looks. Dark eyes, almost violet. I didn't see it until he pointed it out, but it's true."

Her hand brushes my hair back. "I told him nothing about you, of course. But he wants to know if you would agree to meet with him."

I search Marilyn's face. Her eyes narrow over the top of her glasses. I think about her meetings with other girls, which I thought were mother-daughter chats.

"He just wants to meet you." She spreads her hands in the air, as if to say my suspicion's unfounded. "Andrea, I run this club on the up and up. I'm just trying to help you. Marriage has been the best thing in the world for me." She twists her thick gold wedding band as she says this. "Sometimes, if you wait, you lose the opportunity."

"Troy and I are rock solid," I say. "We could wait forever if we had to, but we'd rather get started on our life now."

Marilyn smiles as if she knows I'm lying.

"He's willing to pay just to meet me?"

"A hundred dollars. No touching," she says.

I look through the one-way mirror to the stage. The technician is fiddling with the foot lights. The velvet curtain ripples in light and shadow, mauve in the light and something deeper in the shadow. Behind the curtain, the other dancers are helping each other with outfits and makeup and maybe a small amount of a substance to bolster their courage. I remember why I took this job—so Troy and I could get started on a new life together.

"I need two hundred," I say. "Where do we meet?"

"Right here," Marilyn says. "It's safe. I'll call and arrange for him to meet you after your shift tonight, and I'll keep a bouncer on duty until your fiancé picks you up. You won't need to ask for the money, he'll put it on the desk. Let him talk to you about his wife. After half an hour, look at the clock. He'll know that it's time to go. Lock the door and then," she stands and goes to the door I always thought was a closet, "you can shower and be ready to get married when your fiancé picks you up."

A shower in her office? I can or should reconsider, but suddenly the idea of marrying Troy now, before things fall apart, means more than anything else. "That's fantastic," I say.

Marilyn opens the door to show me out with the same finality I imagine using with this man—she leans forward with her body and her gaze, as if she's already on to the next thing.

"Just one thing, Marilyn. What's his name?"

She looks over my head as she says, "Mr. Hansen."

Code name, I think. I thank her and hurry back stage. Tonight, my place is by the pole, and I start with the usual moves—I'm a very mechanical dancer, I admit—but all of a sudden I'm bumping and grinding with feeling, holding the empty holster. I hear beyond the music the voices of men whistling and murmuring, and I know I'm the one they watch tonight. For the first time in my life, I believe I'm really beautiful. I move closer to them—they yell more. At the end of our shift, the other girls say, "You got the moves now, Andrea," and "Girl, you hot tonight."

Their words are friendship, more meaningful than the guys' catcalls, and I feel such a bond with them as I watch them change from their satin and lace and fringe back to their jeans and coats. They look like regular girls again, except more beautiful. When they ask why I'm not getting changed, I tell them I'm working a double, which is only a half-lie. I wait for them to clear out, and then I walk down the hall to Marilyn's office and open the door quick, before I can change my mind. The first thing I see is my reflection in the mirror; the thigh boots make me look tall. A white envelope sits on Marilyn's desk. Mr. Hansen, gray haired and neatly groomed with a navy blazer and blue polo shirt, stands up. His eyes shine with tears. The guy really lost his wife.

"Remarkable," he whispers.

"Your wife's name was Eileen?"

He nods and gently squeezes my hand, then releases it. "How did she die?"

"Cancer," he said. "Thyroid. But, if it's not too rude, may I ask you not to talk for a moment? Your voice is so young. When you talk, I can't see or feel her at all." He holds his hands, trembling like hurt animals.

I touch them.

"No, no," he says. "You mustn't."

I take my hand away.

"That beautiful profile. Those cheekbones. But it's in the eyes I see her. They have that same aged pain. I don't know how you got that so young."

I want to cry and tell him about my mother, but as he's requested, I don't talk. I swallow back my tears. He pulls a handkerchief from his pocket. *A handkerchief for God's sake*, I think. *Who uses those things anymore?* It smells like expensive men's aftershave, and I dab my cheeks only lightly. I don't want Troy to smell that.

Mr. Hansen, if this is his real name, stuffs the used hanky in his pocket and says, "This will seem odd and if you agree, of course I will compensate you more, but Eileen and I loved to dance. We danced all over the world in some of the most romantic hotels. Would you dance with me, Andrea?"

I hesitate. Dancing is what I do for a living, but what do I know of waltzes and fox trots? Nothing. I tell him this.

"I'll lead," he taps his heart as if somehow it were connected to the dancing.

I think of Troy. "Okay," I shrug. "Let's dance."

He stands and holds his arms out from his body in a formal way. I put my arms in his. Our bodies do not touch. His feet guide mine. We start to move so lightly I no longer feel tired, so light and smooth I think someone else is moving us on a carousel floor. He hums something I remember from high school music, "The Blue Danube," and round and round we go, the image of me in the mirror, dressed in leather boots and holster. I close my eyes.

Suddenly, he stops. "It's not right," he mutters. "Eileen always wore a scarf—it would flow out," he moves his arm like a wing. "So graceful… Would you mind?" He pulls out a long white scarf from his pocket and offers it to me. The first thing I think is that he'll strangle me, but his eyes shine too bright to be violent. I wrap the scarf so one end flows down my back and I take off the holster. We start again, creating invisible squares on Marilyn's carpet.

"Oh, Eileen. Eileen," he sobs. Imagine loving someone that much. I think of Mr. Troy Germaine, my husband-to-be. When the song is finished, Mr. Hansen drops two more hundred-dollar bills into the envelope on the desk and goes to the door.

"Goodbye, my dear," he says. I hand him his scarf. He kisses it, then stuffs it in his pocket and closes the door behind him.

I have hours to wait for Troy. I think of poor Mr. Hansen, missing his wife so much that he would pay hundreds of dollars just to dance with someone who looks like her. When two people love each other, somebody always ends up alone, with a hole in the heart. It's risky. Troy and I are young though, just starting out, and I don't want to think about what the end will be like. I doze a while on Marilyn's couch, then shower and dress.

The engine of the Nova clanks miserably coming up the driveway to the back entrance of the club where dancers must exit. Tim, the bouncer, escorts me out.

"Have a good day, sweetie," he says as he always does.

"I will. I'm getting married today."

He gives me a thumbs-up and disappears back into the club.

I climb into the Nova, wearing a white lace blouse with silver buttons, a flowered blue skirt, and a pair of silver heels.

Troy whistles and hands me a white rose. "Within the hour, you will be Mrs. Troy Germaine," he says.

"Mrs. Troy Germaine," I repeat and lean over and kiss him. Then I unwrap the bagel, cheese, and fruit he packed. He tries to make sure I get my basic food groups.

Troy watches me eat then asks, "What's that you're singing?"

I stop. "Marilyn gave us a wedding present." I flash the wad of money. "For a nice room and a fancy meal with shrimp and crab and a bottle of champagne. Non-alcoholic, of course."

Troy hits the gas. "I promise to love you forever, beautiful," he says. We reach the courthouse by nine, park under a row of pecan trees with their nutty fragrance, and climb the imposing steps with all the workers dressed in suits and ties. We find the office, with its shiny glass panel set into the door. There I see the image of two young and beautiful people, looking excited and a little nervous. A sign over the door reads, "Marriage and Firearm Licenses Sold Here." I think about the men whistling and hooting when I pretended to drag a gun out of my holster and how glad Mr. Hansen seemed when I removed it. I squeeze Troy's hand and together we go through the door so we can become husband and wife.

Destiny's Appearance

The day the boy rode into Asheville, a tropical storm was whipping up the coast from Louisiana. Radio announcers in Connecticut cautioned people to stay off the roads even before one drop of rain fell, but Earl Roy and his wife, Marilyn, were not about to close their country western bar—River Star Ranch—just because of a storm, especially not on the day of River Star Ranch's annual Star Search.

They were at the bar that morning when the boy opened the door and the wind whipped in behind him. Marilyn looked past him out into the parking lot, where his old Chevy pickup sat, rounded fenders, rusty runners, dents and all. His truck, his worn blue jeans and scuffed cowboy boots, even the way he filled the doorframe, was curious.

He glanced at her and smiled. "I want to sing tonight."

Just then, the sky started to rumble and rain pelted the ground, sending dust into the air outside. Marilyn pulled the boy in and shut the door behind him. His hand was warm and dry, like an electric blanket, and Marilyn could feel the electricity running. His eyes lit on Earl coming toward them.

"I guess this storm's going to be a humdinger," Earl said to Marilyn. "They say it's veering inland, coming our way."

The boy focused on Earl, and Marilyn saw his china doll beauty, the blond hair, clear skin, and periwinkle blue eyes narrow to an almost animal alertness.

Earl looked at Marilyn.

"He wants to sing," she said.

"Is that so?" Earl looked hard at the boy.

"Yes, sir."

Thunder shook the air. Both Earl and Marilyn jumped, but the boy didn't flinch.

Earl tipped his head to the side, as if changing perspective would help him figure the boy out. "I'm sorry. We get only name bands, top performers for this competition. People pay sixteen bucks a ticket or more to get in here."

"That's what I'm going to be." The boy turned to the almost empty room. "One of the best. I can fill this house now, I bet."

"What's your name?"

"Jamie Fillmore."

"Jamie Fillmore," Earl repeated. "All due respect, son, but I never heard of you and I know most people in the business if they're that good. You're telling me you can fill this house?"

The boy nodded.

Earl plunked the armful of linens he was holding onto the table. "Alright then, let's have one song. Make it your best." He eased himself into a chair. Marilyn sat next to him.

"Doesn't matter what I play," the boy said as he opened his guitar case. "They all sound good." He pulled out a shiny red and white guitar.

Marilyn smiled. "You are full of piss and vinegar! You remind me of my husband." She nudged Earl's leg, but Earl was watching the boy. "You go ahead and sing for me and I'll give you a plate of ribs, on the house."

Jamie tossed his head, fit the strap over his shoulder, and plucked a few strings of the guitar. He opened his mouth and started to sing.

Earl's arm slipped off the back of Marilyn's chair as the boy's mouth emitted sound like a blast of wind forced through a winding tunnel of rock. And the wind—his voice—was like antiquity. It riveted Earl to his seat. He didn't know the song; he wasn't paying attention to the words. He listened to the voice. The boy's voice came rushing on the air high and low pitched, free and focused at the same time.

Earl's face turned fish-belly white and sweat broke out above his lip. That boy had a voice as pure as only one other voice he'd ever heard. It was old as rock and young as new breath, and borne up by a spirit not of this world. The boy knew he held power over both of them, but it was Earl he watched. When he finished singing, he took a slight bow.

"Boy," Earl cleared his throat and the word came out as a growl. "Where'd you get a singing voice like that?"

"It's in the family," Jamie said.

Earl sat back, mouth open and shook his head.

Marilyn touched his shoulder. "Earl? Earl? Are you alright?"

Earl didn't speak. He couldn't speak. He wasn't there. He was in the hot New Orleans sun, in a fallow field of cotton, the magnificent pecan trees waving in the wind; Spanish moss draped from each like a lacy shawl on a ghost. Earl gulped down some air. "Yes," he croaked.

Marilyn shifted her attention from Earl back to Jamie. "Your family must be so proud of you."

"My mother died a few months ago. Pancreatic cancer." Now his eyes were moist with tears; but behind the tears, they were clear.

Earl winced.

"Oh, that's an awful thing for a boy your age," Marilyn crooned. She wasn't looking at Earl—she was thinking of her own children, surrendered to her first husband because she had messed up, not through abuse, but neglect. She had neglected herself and they were the collateral damage. They were old enough now for the scars to show. But it seemed they didn't think they had scars as long as she stayed out of their lives. She had tried to win them back, but they weren't interested. She didn't even know what they looked like now. "How old are you, Jamie?"

"Eighteen," he answered. Her own son was just eighteen.

"Your daddy?" Earl leaned toward the boy. "What about him?"

"Never knew him," Jamie replied.

Marilyn put her hand on Earl's arm. "Earl, can we put him on the roster?"

Earl squirmed on his chair like he was sitting on a hundred volts. He rubbed his hands on his thighs. "Alright, then. Come back at six o'clock."

Jamie nodded and put away his guitar. He turned to leave.

"Jamie," Earl called him back. "How did you know about Star Search?"

The boy's eyes narrowed. "You're a name in the industry, sir."

Earl puffed up. "I used to be. In New Orleans. Then I met Marilyn, and I had to save her from her evil ways." He smirked but hurt washed over Marilyn's face.

She kept her voice light and replied "Earl, I have been saved by a higher power than capital Y-O-U."

Earl smiled at her, a tight little smile. "I don't think so, Marilyn."

"I know so." Marilyn shook her head to wipe away the pain, then smiled bravely at the boy. "Earl had a place on Bourbon Street," she said with pride.

"You heard of Bourbon Street?" Earl shot at Jamie.

"Sir, I was born on Bourbon Street." Jamie turned away again.

Marilyn followed him to the door. Looking back, she saw Earl staring after the boy. The lunch crowd had begun to appear, needing her attention.

Earl was still there, sitting in his trance.

"Hey, Marilyn!" the cook shouted. "Maybe you'd like to take out these plates?"

Marilyn rushed to the kitchen, grabbed the entrees, and took them out, leaning over to kiss Earl on the head as she passed by. He moved out from under the caress of her lips. She found him a few minutes later in the supply room, stacking linens.

"Earl, what are you doing in here? You've got to get to the bank and get the prize check before noon." It was like he was sleepwalking. She poked him. "Hon, you hear me?"

"Stop nagging me." He put the linens down and pulled his keys from his pocket, but she was standing in the doorway. "I'll be back in an hour."

They had been married for eighteen years, sixteen of them in Asheville. They moved up north and opened River Star Ranch, where just one ghost had continued to haunt him. It had taken him years to reconcile himself to this place, to the smallness of it compared to Bourbon Street. But now here was this boy, and the storm, stirring up his memory.

Marilyn stood under the light and Earl noticed with distaste the gray roots of her hair and the sagging skin under her chin. She took a deep breath. "I don't know why you say things to hurt me, Earl, but I'm not going to try to hurt you back. I know you've got disappointments. We all get disappointed in life, but that doesn't mean you just pass it on, especially to the person who loves you."

That was classic Marilyn. She laid her vulnerability at his feet for him to step on or respect. He saw she had prepared his "stage outfit," as she called it—silver-studded belt, his cowboy hat, and a checked shirt—pressed and neatly folded on a shelf next to the old red cowboy boot from which he would draw the winner's name.

When Earl looked back to the door, the space Marilyn had occupied was empty.

"I know your mother's name," he whispered to the empty room. "Her name is Alyson Brand."

Earl's bar had been on Bourbon Street. He waited for the time of day when the music started, when he could stand on the uneven sidewalk and hear the air fill with its music. The saxophones, trumpets, drums like spirits filling the sky, swirling overhead, swooping down to enter his bar, his ears, his soul. The music was his joy.

And that was how he met Alyson Brand. She was with a group coming through New Orleans for a month. That first night, she sang and he heard her voice, the same voice as the boy's now—exactly that voice without gender, not owned by sex, unfettered from the world. His whole life had prepared him for her because he expected love to come like a thunder bolt, not low and grounded and quiet, as it had with Marilyn. He and Marilyn had been married for one unremarkable year. As soon as he saw Alyson, with her platinum hair scooped up and held by a clip in the back, except for a few wispy strands that hung down and caressed her neck and then heard her sing, he fell in love. That first night after her gig they closed his bar and still found places to go.

"I should go back to the hotel and rest my voice," she said. It was nearly eight in the morning. Instead, they walked to Café Du Monde, where a swarm of people gathered under the canopy in Jackson Square, voices animated and happy. The waiter brought them chicory coffee and a plate of hot beignets with powdered sugar heaped on top, and Earl and Alyson watched the birds swoosh down to the empty tables and peck at the sugary crumbs. By nine o'clock, the jazz started and voices rose and fell with the beat. He liked the way Alyson tossed her head, like she was shaking the music around all the time. A saxophone player had played "Smile and the World Smiles with You," and Alyson had sung along. All talking stopped. All eyes were on her. Earl felt proud to be with her.

The month had gone by in a blur. She was twenty-eight to his forty-three. Every night, he listened to her sing and every day, he shared all the people in his life with her, including all the music connections. Earl hardly went home, and it wasn't long before Marilyn knew of the affair, but Earl didn't care. He had never felt so alive, so connected to a purpose, a reason for doing everything he did, every minute of the day… and night. He took Alyson to the best bars, the places where important people played.

One night after hot music and hotter sex, they lay in her hotel room watching the sun come up and Earl said, "This weekend, I'm going to tell Marilyn I'm leaving her."

"What?" Alyson shook her head, her objection clear. "Why?"

"Because of us? For us." He reached for her hand.

She pushed him away. "We never talked about this. I'm going to Nashville, Earl. This is… Well, this is just what it is."

He saw then that she thought she was poised on the edge of greatness, stretching into her future success and leaving him far in the background.

"But you'll need a home to come back to, wherever you go." He hated how weak he sounded but he said it anyway. He couldn't lose her.

She flung his arm off her and sprang off the bed. The next day, she left New Orleans and every day, he waited for her to return. He waited for months on end. Marilyn hovered over him, but he wouldn't speak about it. How could Alyson disappear after she had made him love her like that, plan his whole life around her? She was like fog lifting off the road during a rainstorm. She was night itself. But still, he waited for her to come back. His business faltered. Alyson cut a record, and it sold but not well. He thought she might come back then. No. More months stretched on. Then Marilyn's uncle died, and she inherited the house in Asheville. She told him she was leaving and he needed to make a choice. He didn't see it as much of a choice. He felt dead either way.

What if—? Now, Earl knew this might sound crazy, but not so crazy. What if this boy was his son? He and Marilyn had not had any children together. What if Alyson had gone off and had this baby and never wanted to tell him—who knew why. But it would be like her. Why else would this boy be here now? He wanted to believe this boy was family.

Marilyn waited for him to leave for the bank, and then she slipped away from the lunch crowd, into the back room, and locked the door. She sank down onto the floor, and slowed her breath. The storm had kicked up again, the wind whining and crying like a baby. Just like a baby, stuck alone in some room, whining and crying. Marilyn started to cry, remembering how her children had clung to her when Family Services came to take them away. They were so young. She was just twenty-two, and the kids were two and three. She had tried to stop drinking after the kids were born. Her first husband had given her chances—she couldn't say he hadn't. She went to rehab after Family Services took the kids. She intended to get them back. She found a halfway house, relapsed, went to rehab again and then got a job waitressing. That's where she met Earl. It was true, in a sense, that his stability saved her sanity in those earlier days. But that was *before*, as she referred to it. *After*, forgiving him had become practice for forgiving herself. Still, there were days, like this one, when she wondered why she bothered.

At 5:30, the sky was pitch black. The storm thrashed and moaned, but River Star Ranch was filling up for Star Search. Many of the singers were going to be late. The storm had delayed flights and downed power lines had prevented others from getting there and Earl was in a foul mood. That last day he had seen Alyson, a tropical storm blew through New Orleans and now, this boy appeared in a storm with a voice just like hers.

Now Jamie was wearing a black cowboy hat pulled low over his eyes. Earl and Marilyn approached him at the entrance from opposite sides of the restaurant. Earl reached him first.

"A bunch of people on the roster are stuck in traffic. Can you sing?"

Jamie looked into the restaurant and his face was a screen, but when he nodded, Earl could see her profile again—the aquiline nose, the straight brows, the chiseled chin.

"Was Alyson Brand your mother?" He blurted it out.

"Who?" Jamie frowned.

"Are you serious, Earl?" Marilyn asked. "After all these years—?"

The boy's gaze went between the two of them. Earl was still convinced that the boy was his son.

Marilyn stepped back and dropped the plate of ribs she was carrying.

"You don't deserve me, Earl. You never really forgot about her, did you?" She spun away.

"Marilyn, come back here," Earl tried, but Marilyn kept walking so he grabbed a broom, swept up the mess, and tossed it in the garbage.

Jamie adjusted his hat on his head.

Thunder split the silence; the lights flickered and went out.

"Shit," Earl muttered. In the pitch black, he could see nothing. "Stay seated everyone. Give me two minutes to get to the basement and turn on the generator." He lowered his voice and whispered, "Jamie? Can you sing for them? Something to keep them occupied so they don't panic?"

"Sure thing, sir," Jamie answered.

Earl clapped his hands together. "Please. Mr. Jamie Fillmore is going to sing for you while I go start the generator." Earl backed away, arms reaching for the wall behind him. Plunged into the dark, his other senses kicked in. He found the door and eased his way down the stairs and around the wall to the generator. In the pitch dark, he felt bad about uttering Alyson's name. "Who?" the boy had asked. Did he really not know? Earl saw again in his mind's eye how Marilyn had flinched at the mention of Alyson's name. It hadn't been uttered in all the years they'd been in Connecticut. Before he flipped the switch and heard the familiar hum of electricity, just for a moment, he paused to listen to the boy's voice. While beautiful and pure, it no longer sounded like the voice he remembered. It sounded tinny now, like an adolescent's undeveloped soprano. Why had he thought otherwise? How had that voice held such power earlier? Was it Destiny itself, come to correct his memory? He was having trouble breathing. He could hear Marilyn crying in the back hallway.

He started the generator and light flooded the basement. Pushing open the doors of the bulkhead, he scrambled up the steps and let the rain pelt him. There was no moon, but outside he could breathe. By the light of the floodlights he followed the stone walk to the front door of the restaurant. He could see Jamie singing now. Through the window, he could see that the boy was standing in the center of the room, holding the microphone, turning each time he sang a few phrases. He sang as if the entire room was his stage. The people clapped, and Earl saw the joy on the boy's face, a face that no longer looked like Alyson's. This Jamie Fillmore, who lit the room, was a stranger to him.

Marilyn came and stood in the corner of the room, wiping her face with a dishtowel. Her white shirt cast her skin in a sallow light, showing the dark circles beneath her eyes. She smiled bravely at the boy. Earl saw how tired she looked; he had to acknowledge her hard work kept everything going, and she did it not because she loved it, but because she loved him. She closed her eyes and moved her lips. Was she praying?

He began to see himself through her eyes—haunted by the ghost of a memory of a woman who had never loved him, who had used all his musical connections and disappeared from his life, while his wife had taken him back, forgiven him, and worked by his side to make his dream a reality for all these years. What a terrible betrayal of her love he had committed. Lights swung into the parking light behind him, one of the bands arriving.

He moved toward the door.

Marilyn's eyes fluttered open and she glanced out the window and saw him, soaking wet. She pulled a cloth from the table and met him at the door with it. "You'll catch a death of a cold," she said.

"You're right," Earl said, catching her hand. "I don't deserve you, Marilyn. I mean it."

"I know." She smiled and patted him with the cloth again. "You think I don't know? Go on in now, Earl. Tell them the first band is here."

She shoved him into the dining room, and all the people turned toward him. Jamie was still holding the microphone. Earl plucked it out of his hands.

"I'd like you all to give a hand to Jamie." The crowd obliged. "That's some voice on that boy. I'm sure you'll get to be that star you're planning on becoming."

The door opened, and their lead act walked in. Earl looked around at the people. He saw young Willie and his girlfriend, Cheryl, dressed up for an evening out, and some of the old timers, like Useless John, scattered amongst the newcomers, people he'd never seen, showing up for the event.

"Just one minute before the band comes on. Tonight, I'd like to acknowledge my wife, Marilyn."

Marilyn stood in the entryway. She waved the dishtowel.

"Honey, it's you holding me together. I'm sure all these people know it. I'm sorry it took me so long to see it." He held his arm out for her and she floated toward him and tucked herself in his embrace, the one she had waited so long for.

Useless John

One hot Saturday morning in June, John Cantera was wakened by the sound of pounding fists on the door of his trailer.

"John! Useless John, damn you! Get yourself up and open this door. I know you're in there."

Big Earl. His southern twang—was it Louisiana? Or Alabama? John couldn't remember, but he loved the way Earl had of stretching words so you went along just to be surprised about where you would end up, like the canoe trip he took down the Shetucket one time.

"Useless John!"

John had been in a deep sleep. He sat up, rubbed his face, and squinted at the wall clock. Ten o'clock. The air conditioner whined, signaling that it was already too hot outside. Sunlight spilled around the edges of the trailer's window blinds. John hadn't seen Earl for a week. For the two of them, that was a big stretch. Earl had taken his wife on vacation to Niagara Falls. He hoped a vacation would get her mind off her desire to buy a bigger house. Earl didn't want to take on any debt. He was sixty-two. His wife was forty-nine. By the tone of Earl's voice, John guessed his friend's plan to diffuse his wife's desire to "upgrade," as he called it, had flopped.

John stood, picked up the afghan that had fallen to the floor, and went to answer Earl's knocks, which had become more insistent.

"Well, it's about time! You been keeping clean?" Earl swooped through the door and came straight at John. He peered into John's eyes. "Good man," he said. Then he straightened himself, or at least as much as he could. He was a big man, over six feet, with an enormous girth. Everything gave way to it except for his belt, which managed, curiously, to stay poised at the middle of his belly. He wore a short-sleeved, button-down shirt wide open at the neck, revealing his fleshy chest and a thick gold chain with a medallion nestled in his chest hair. His blue jeans were pressed with a crease down the middle.

Earl did a visual sweep of the living room and kitchen area where he stood. "When are you ever going to clean this place?" he asked, but John knew Earl was really looking for empty bottles. There were none, and had been none for nine years, but still Earl checked. When John didn't answer, Earl said, "I got a job over in Berlee, needs a new floor today."

"Why the emergency?" John asked, although he didn't have any other plans for the day.

Earl explained his crew had been removing the asbestos linoleum to get to a wide plank pine floor that was original to an 1850s farmhouse. But underneath the linoleum and the subfloor they had been surprised to find more linoleum, this one glued to the hardwood floor with asbestos glue. The asbestos glue made it virtually impossible to salvage the original floor, as it would be dangerous to release the asbestos fibers into the air. Earl moved over to the window and pulled up the blinds as he spoke.

"Poor lady just about cried when we told her she wasn't going to be able to salvage the floor. But I told her I'd come find my floor man and she'd have a floor by the end of the day."

"She's got the materials?"

Earl came back over to where John stood. "How could she have materials if she didn't know she needed a new floor? We'll stop at Home Depot and pick up everything you need." He gave John a playful whack across the back of his head. "It's good to see you, Useless."

"If I'm so useless, how come you just about broke my damned door down to get to me?" John pulled on jeans and a tee shirt. He was still wearing socks from the day before. He jammed his feet into his work boots and pulled the laces tight. Earl was already walking toward the door, dialing his cell phone, which looked like a tiny toy in his oversized fist.

"I found Useless," he was saying. "We're set to go."

They drove to Home Depot and picked out red oak floor planks, already cut in tongue and groove fashion to be snapped and locked together. They collected all the other materials—glue, nails, paper, and loaded everything into Earl's truck. When they climbed back into the truck, John fiddled with the dials, adjusting air vents, the radio station, and his seat. Finally, he cleared his throat. "Today is my ten-year anniversary, Earl."

"Ten years," Earl said. "That's a long time."

"I guess I owe you an awful lot," John said. "I know I do."

Earl pushed his cap back on his head. "Don't you worry about it."

He looked like he intended to go on, but suddenly he slammed on his brakes. Traffic ahead had slowed to a crawl. Whirling lights of service vehicles flashed on both sides of the road.

John gripped his door. "Oh no," he said.

"Take it easy," Earl said. Just ahead, they saw a white pickup truck with its passenger side bashed in. It stretched across two far lanes, facing in the wrong direction. Off to the other side, a little subcompact car, the front end crushed. An EMT crew hovered around the car like bees to a hive. On the ground, a stretcher waited, with the blanket folded down. Another stretcher contained a body bag, zipped up. One ambulance was backing up to the car, while another was pulling away from the truck up ahead. That ambulance merged into traffic, siren wailing, and disappeared from sight, leaving behind only the ghostly wail.

With a quick snap of the wrist, Earl veered off the road.

John gripped the dashboard. "What are you doing?"

"Seeing if we can help." He had the door open before the truck was fully stopped.

"That's ridiculous!" John said, but too late. Earl was already gone.

There was already so much noise, the sirens and the people shouting. The whining Jaws of Life was now cutting the little blue car, sending sparks flying. John saw the cop pointing at Earl, then to the truck. John could see Earl didn't want to go anywhere until he had helped in some way. The cop got angry. His face was red. He stepped toward Earl, jabbing his finger into Earl's chest. Earl finally got the picture. He threw his hands in the air and got back in the truck, slamming the door behind him. He threw the truck into gear and pulled out into the flow of traffic, almost causing another accident.

"In Louisiana, they would have been happy for the help!" he said.

"You've been living here for more than ten years," John said. His hands were still trembling. "You ought to know better."

"What's wrong with you?" Earl shouted. "After your experience you ought to be the first to lend a helping hand."

John didn't bother saying that he was lending a hand—to Earl—or that he knew better than to obstruct the site of an accident. Most people did. He said nothing. Instead, he rolled down the window and leaned out to gulp some fresh air. He peered through the side mirror, trying to see if the EMTs had yet recovered the trapped passenger. But the highway curved and the only thing John could see was his own face, the sandy-colored mustache hiding the down turn of his lips. With a shock, he saw his gaunt cheekbones jutting out, throwing shadows on his pale skin.

"Ten years," Earl said. "Sitting on the sidelines. You might just as well be the one dead, for all the living you do." There was a long moment of silence in the truck, then suddenly the radio sputtered and an advertisement came on.

Between them, they almost never spoke her name. Earl had known Becky first, had hired her as a waitress at River Star Ranch. River Star Ranch was eastern Connecticut's largest country bar and barbeque ribs place. Earl owned it and had built it from a roadside take-out shack. It was his pride and joy. He could count on a crowd of several hundred every weekend. With that kind of turnover, most of the wait staff got burned out fast. But not Becky. She had loved people and they had loved her. When she laughed, every table within earshot stopped talking to hear her laugh float toward them, like a flock of birds rising off a field. John had seen her there when he stopped in with some of his buddies from the construction crew, but he didn't approach her until they both happened to be at the local Knights of Columbus one Friday night, two-stepping. He had asked her if she wanted to go four wheeling on the beach in his Jeep, and she had laughed and asked if he wanted to ride on her motorcycle. They were married two months later in Vegas. They thought they had plenty of time for everything, but before their first anniversary, Becky was dead. At the funeral, John and Earl spoke little.

It was later on, on the one-year anniversary of Becky's death, that their lives connected. John had ended his night of drinking at River Star Ranch. Earl was closing when he found John lying face down in the men's room. He tried to help John stand, and when he did, John promptly threw up all over the floor Earl had just mopped.

He got a good look at him and realized whom he was holding. "You are the most useless man," Earl had proclaimed. Earl took him home and let him sleep on the couch in his basement because Earl had this thing for helping people that went way beyond reason. The next day, John went back to the restaurant and did a little carpentry work for Earl. He had been going back every day for nine years, and Earl had looked out for him since then. The name "Useless John" had stuck, even though over the years John had singlehandedly built an addition, which seated a hundred patrons, a storage shed, a new roof, shutters for twenty windows, and matching window boxes. But his best work was the parquet floor he designed and constructed in the new addition. It was made of alternating maple and cherry inlays, starting with a starburst pattern right smack in the middle and some rays radiating from it. He had copied the pattern from an Amish quilt he and Becky had bought on one of their bike trips to Pennsylvania. The quilt lay in a closet somewhere now. After looking at that floor, Earl had said, "Useless, now I've seen this floor, I know what you were made for."

It was true he was a floor man, but he had never danced on that dance floor and he didn't ever plan to.

Just then, they pulled into a driveway that curved around the side of an old clapboard cape. The boards were stained a dark brown so that they almost blended in color with the trunks of the towering maples and oaks just behind the house. In fact, If John had blinked he could have missed the house, so well did it blend with the background, except for the trim around the windows and front door, which was a warm salmon color. The house sat surrounded on all sides by a moss-covered stone wall, over four feet high and almost as thick. From a break in the front section of the wall, a gate opened in toward the house.

"I want to take a look at this wall," John said, stepping out of the truck. Earl waited for him and then together, they went to the front door. The anger between them had evaporated, as it often did.

"What's this lady's name?" John asked.

"Erma. Erma Shumaker."

John was getting ready to make a wisecrack about the name when the door opened. John stepped back. Becky! His lips began to form her name. It was her. No, it wasn't. The sunlight caught her hair, reddish brown, like the color of cinnamon. It always felt warm to his touch. There were those honey-colored freckles across her chest. And the muscular shoulders, from years of baling hay and lifting buckets of feed to the animals. He longed to rush to her. But no, this woman was not Becky. Her hair was messy and her clothes rumpled, but her words were polished and soft. Not loud and boisterous like Becky.

"It's so nice of you to make the time to do this on such short notice," she said. John still couldn't speak.

Earl stepped into John's line of vision. He looked pleased with himself. "John, this is Erma Shumaker. Erma, this here's the best floor man in the state of Connecticut."

She reached out her hand and grasped his firmly. "Thank you," she said. "Really, I do appreciate it. My son is asthmatic, and I thought I would get this done while he's visiting his father. You know, because of the dust. But now, we've got quite a mess here." She gestured for him to follow her through the makeshift "shower," a room made of wide polyurethane strips nailed to the walls as a precursor to the asbestos removal. She led the way through the front room, toward the kitchen. The narrow hallway accentuated her wide hips, which had a graceful sway to them. They had to step through more long panels of polyurethane plastic that the containment crew was now beginning to dissemble in the kitchen. The room was bright yellow. Sunlight flooded through the curtain-less windows.

"Here it is," she said, her hand sweeping wide open.

John couldn't help but notice her chest, big like Becky's. "You've got good light here," he said.

"Yes, I love it too," she said, and now her face wrinkled with concern. "Will the new floor make it dark in here?"

"No, ma'am." Earl grinned. "John here's an artist. Just wait." He disappeared back through the polyurethane "door" with the containment crew and left the two of them alone. Erma regarded John.

"You have windows north and south," John explained, thinking she was waiting for a more thorough answer to her question, "so you must get sun all day."

"That's right," she said. "I do."

"The red oak will give it a glow," he said. "The lighter colors would have made a glare."

"I never would have guessed that." Erma seemed relieved, but then the frown was back. "I wasn't prepared for this extra expense. How much will this cost?"

The way she stood, with her arms out, as if appealing for help, reminded him of the way Becky used to reach for him in the morning. He never lingered in bed now. John looked around the room. It was stripped of all personal touches. He could tell very little about this woman, except by her personal demeanor. He could see that Earl was right. The floor problem had thrown her. She looked like a person easily thrown.

"Let me measure it," John said. He took his tape measure off his belt and gestured for her to hold it while he held the other end. He stooped to the floor and as he stood up, he saw that she was watching him, her eyes moving over his body.

"That's twelve feet, six inches one way," he said. He saw her eyes move over his chest. "You can let go of the tape now," he said.

She took a step back and let the tape measure go. He took out a small pad, wrote down the numbers, and asked her to hold the tape again. He measured the opposite wall and took out his calculator.

"Funny, how you take a floor for granted until something like this happens," she said.

"Oh, don't you worry. We'll get you fixed up in no time."

"That's good." Erma smiled for the first time, a hesitant smile. Not like Becky at all.

"The room's twelve by nine," John said, calculating out loud for her benefit. "That's a hundred and eight square feet. At five dollars per square foot, that's five hundred, forty dollars for labor, plus your materials on top of that."

"We spent nine-eighty on materials," Earl said coming up behind him. "Here's the receipt."

"That's fine," Erma said, switching her gaze from John to Earl. She asked Earl if he would take a check.

John excused himself and went out to the truck. The sun was hot. Sweat dripped down his face. He began unloading the supplies into the garage, where there were two saw horses already set up for him. He got the electric circular saw out of the truck, found an outlet in the garage, plugged in the extension cord and waited for Earl to come along. He took a few deep breaths. He hadn't eaten any breakfast. He felt a bit weak. How could it be possible? At first glance, this woman looked so much like Becky. He groaned inwardly. He'd thought he had felt the worst of it; years of pain flooded back. The containment crew came out of the house. They consisted of three Mexicans who spoke very little English and their supervisor, Little Herman. Little Herman was taller than Earl, and wider, which was hard to imagine until you saw him. He had been raised in the north and had no accent.

"What you up to, John?" Little Herman asked.

"Guess I'm puttin' in this floor today."

"That's what the old man was hoping. We wasted half a day's work, not being able to tear up this linoleum." Little Herman had to duck to enter the garage. "Got to take my crew and go over to the other work site in Voluntown. See if we can turn any kind of profit today."

John nodded. He didn't like Little Herman's more calculating sense of profit, but he understood it could be frustrating to be in business with Earl, who had the restaurant to make his living. If the asbestos removal business generated enough money for him to keep River Star Ranch going, Earl was a happy man. Some of the country singers cost eight thousand dollars a gig.

Just then, Earl came out of the house with Erma. The workers were drinking water out of a garden hose and Erma went over to them. "Not that water, please. It's so stale. Let me get you something to drink. I have juice and bottled water." She and the men regarded each other.

Finally, one of them said, "Soda?"

"Let me check." Erma sashayed into the house, her hair and her hips bouncing. She came back with three cans. "I'm sorry," she said. "I have just one soda." She held up the other two cans. "Seltzer water?" She looked at Little Herman.

He spoke to the workers in Spanish. They shrugged and took the cans. Erma watched them drink for a moment.

"Ain't she a ticket?" Earl chuckled, coming up to stand near John. He slapped his hat back on his head. "I've got to go see about that other crew we've got in Voluntown." Earl took out his cell phone and studied the analog face of it. "What time you figure you'll be done here?"

John could see the time was already 12:30. "Seven, maybe later." He shifted his attention back to Erma, still standing near Herman.

"You have a good crew," Erma was saying. "I'm sorry it worked out this way." She thanked Herman and the men and shook their hands before they got back into the truck. Earl got into his own truck and pulled out behind them, giving a brief wave to John.

The first two hours passed quickly. John pulled off the molding around the existing floor, measured the first few boards, cut them, and then nailed them down. The room was not quite square, so as he reached the middle of the floor, he had to measure one board at a time. During that time, he didn't see Erma, but once just as he finished nailing down a section, he heard her on the phone.

"I told you... if he comes home now... Can't you be just a little bit flexible? No. He'll have a full-fledged attack. How could I have known? One extra night.... Fine! Let me talk to him." Then her voice smoothed over and got low enough so he couldn't hear the words. A few moments later, he heard the vacuum upstairs and then her moving about through the rooms, the floor boards creaking.

John focused on his work. He saw only the wood and the dust as it settled over him, on his shoes, his pants, his skin, in his nostrils. He lost himself in the task, in the rhythm of it, in the acid smell and taste of the fiber, until her shadow crossed over him while he was bent over the saw. She had changed her clothes now. She had traded the tight tee shirt for a paper-thin pink cotton oxford—John could see a black stretchy bra underneath. She also wore a pair of sweat pants that were worn to the point of holes. He shifted his gaze to her face. Her eyes were red.

"Are you thirsty?" she asked. "I made some lemonade."

John shook his head. "I better keep going if I'm going to get this floor finished today."

"I always thought my husband and I would uncover that floor together."

John stopped his work to let her go on.

She shrugged and looked off toward the woods. "After we divorced, I thought, well, I'll just do it myself." She shook her head and smiled. "I always think I can do everything myself. I started to tear up the linoleum and someone told me I better check for asbestos, so I did and wouldn't you know, it was loaded. One thing led to another . . . and now we have a big mess. How stupid."

"Nothing stupid about wanting to do for yourself," he said.

Just then the phone rang.

"Don't you want to get that?" he asked.

"Not really." She frowned, but when the phone went on ringing, she went to answer. In a moment she was back. "It's for you," she said.

He switched off the saw and took the cordless unit from her. Earl's voice came booming through the receiver.

"Yep, well, no. I'm about halfway, but the thresholds will slow me up some. I might have to cut the doors some. Well, maybe not till midnight if you keep interrupting me, Earl. You like that phone too much." He handed the phone back to Erma and picked up another piece of wood.

She stood watching him for a moment. Then she said, "Earl asked for Useless."

Instead of answering, John turned on the saw and set the piece of oak snug up against the blade. He felt relieved when the blade bit into the wood and pulled it hungrily to its teeth. The excess dropped to the ground. She was still standing there, watching him.

He blew on the cut edge and dust scattered in a fan outward.

"I got no complaint with Earl," he said. "He's been like a father to me."

She took a sip of the glass of lemonade she'd carried with her into the room.

Suddenly, he was thirsty. "I guess I will take some of that lemonade," he said. He carried the board past her, into the house, and fit it snug against the others. He pressed the nail gun and shot the nails into the under lip of the wood, making it fast. She followed him, got a glass from the cupboard and poured him some lemonade. He drank it with a few deep gulps and still felt thirsty. She stepped closer and poured him some more.

"You two go back a long way?" she asked.

John took another sip of lemonade. He shattered a piece of ice between his teeth. "Yes, ma'am. Feels like a lifetime." He handed her the glass. "Thank you for the drink. I better get back to work."

He banged his shoulder in his hurry to get back to the garage. Something made him want to speak frankly to her and run away at the same time. He began to push the boards through in a hurry. Several split. He tossed them aside. She would not know that it was due to his carelessness. The sun had started to slant off to the west. "Stupid woman," he muttered. "Stupid woman."

He started to count the boards now. One. Two. Three. How many more? How many more? In the whirr and whine of the saw he heard screeching, then the scream—that scream that had followed him through so many years. A full-throated scream, one that started deep in the belly. A terror scream, then silence. He was losing his breath. He panted and choked on the dust.

He coughed and coughed.

They were not that drunk. Just a few beers, no more than three. He could have walked any line. Passed a breathalyzer if they'd given him one. It wasn't the booze. It was the gigantic pothole in the road. She wasn't wearing her seatbelt. The window was open. A night in June, warm and foggy. Suddenly, the truck was tumbling, and her scream filled the cab and then she was gone. "Becky! Becky!" He called her. That, too, had stayed with him, him screaming her name and not even recognizing his own voice or the act of screaming. And then the metal crash, the glass shattering—but underneath that noise, the silence, the sickening silence. He knew she was dead before he got out, before the paramedics arrived. All that long stretch of minutes, straight to eternity. Becky! Her hair concealing the rock and the blood until he touched her and then it stained his hands. Becky, gone. For ten years, booze or no booze, floors or no floors. He was useless. The tears were there suddenly, like water in a dry riverbed, unlikely and miraculous.

Erma came back outside. He turned away, pretending to measure boards until he believed his eyes were dry. Then he turned toward the door, but she was gone. Good. He could smell himself, the dank sweat, the stink of his own peculiar wound. So much lost. Once he thought of the future, made plans, but now he marched like a pile of bones. Dusk had begun to fall. Where the hell was Earl? He took the cut board into the house and nailed it down. The floor was taking shape. Beautiful red oak. It glowed red in the dusk. Blood. That's what it looked like in the light of the dusky night. He thought he could hear music wafting on the air, strange music. He strained to hear. Indian wailing. Human chanting. He glanced into the living room and saw her stretched out on the floor, arms spread out from her body. *Oh, my God!* He rushed nearer to her and then stopped.

She tipped her head back and expelled air from deep in her belly. Her voice sounded like a gong as she did so, full of vibrations. He knew he shouldn't be watching her, but he couldn't help it. She stretched back on the mat and suddenly arched up, her pelvis tilted in the air. No words. Then down on the floor again. She hugged her knees and sat up. "I do these exercises to relax," she said. "I don't know why I bother."

He shook his head, but he knew he must speak. "I thought you were hurt," he said. He saw the exercise mat. Stretching—she was stretching her body. He wanted to weep. He remembered the way Becky's body surrendered to death. He remembered too much, how he had slumped by that rock waiting while the rain mixed with his tears. She had been driving. That's what he told the police, He couldn't remember anything else, he told them. In the end, their conviction mattered very little to him. He had his own. Because of him, Becky was dead.

He looked down and saw that Erma was crying. He sat down next to her. "Are you alright?" he asked.

She nodded and tried to wipe away the tears.

He patted the floor. It was a wide-plank pine floor, old and full of scratches. He ran his hand over it. "This is a soft floor," he said. "But it's lasted a hundred fifty years. They don't make them this way anymore."

"Is it a good floor you're putting in for me?" she asked.

"It's okay wood," he said, looking into the kitchen, where the red of the grain glowed in the evening light. "Middle of the road quality. I nailed it, so that helps stabilize it."

She laughed suddenly. "Men! They always want to nail things down.... Why do you like to build floors?" she asked.

"Each one is so different," he said. "I like different things about them. Red oak, soft pine, marble, slate. Alone, one piece doesn't look like much, but together, you got something beautiful." He paused. "One thing's the same no matter what material you use: once you fit the floor together tight and snug all the way around, you leave a quarter inch both top and side to breathe."

"Sounds like a person," she said.

He nodded thoughtfully. "I think floors are alive. That's why I prefer natural materials, not linoleum or carpet or that Pergo crap. Pergo—it peels if you do anything close to living a life. People think they can trick it, put down throw rugs at the stress points, but you can't trick a floor." He rapped his knuckles on the soft pinewood. "If you live on it, it wears."

She studied him carefully. "Why do you let Earl call you Useless?"

John caught his breath. The sun was fully down now. Where had the day gone? Earl should be along shortly. The floor wasn't finished. It was the first time John had not finished a job on time.

"Ten years ago, I was in a car accident with my wife. I was driving, and she was thrown from the truck. She died." His voice, so measured and matter of fact, covered all his emotion.

"Oh, my God. I'm sorry to hear that," Erma said.

"You look like her," John said. "When I first saw you—" He averted his eyes and gazed out the window. He did not want her to see what he was thinking or feeling. "She was full of life," he finished.

"I'll take that as a compliment." Now she smiled, not a victorious or gloating smile, but one that suffused her whole face with kindness. "I could sense something about you... a depth, I guess." She uncrossed her legs.

He was not touching her, yet the heat of her had traveled through his own body, up his arm, gushed at the heart and tumbled down to his groin, where it sat. He saw that the color of her eyes was green like moss growing on the stone wall, light one moment, dark the next.

"My wife's name was Becky. She loved to dance." John told her about the dance floor at River Star Ranch.

"That sounds lovely," Erma said. "I'd love to see it sometime."

He looked away. He didn't want to share Becky's floor with her, although every week hundreds of people danced on it. "Maybe you'd like to fit a few of these boards together?" he asked.

"Really?" A light came into her eyes. She scrambled to her feet and stood waiting for him. Together, they went out into the kitchen and he took out his tape measure.

"You've got three-inch boards," he said, "and a room that's not square. So measure here and three inches over." He held the measure at one end and waited while she called out the numbers, then he took her out to the garage and showed her how to measure and mark the next board. Her whole body bent eagerly to the task.

"You've got to tie your hair back before we use the saw," he said. She reached into her pocket, fished out a rubber band, and secured her hair. With her hair fastened, she did not look like Becky. He saw more clearly the tiny lines around her eyes and mouth. She was not young. He explained the saw and how to hold the wood with her thumb folded into her palm so that she didn't get it under the blade. She cut without hesitation. They took the board in and he showed her how to lock it into place. When he picked up the nail gun to move it into place she said, "Can I do it?" so he showed her how to position the gun just so and shoot the nails through the lip. She didn't flinch at the sound.

"Let's do another," she said, so they did, working without words until finally she was measuring and sawing, and he was nailing the boards down. Soon, they were at the end of the room, the threshold area.

"This is called the nosing," John said, holding the fat, thick board with a profile that did indeed look like a nose. "It's a bit tricky."

"You better do that, then," she said.

John looked outside. It was dark now. Where was Earl? For a while, he had forgotten about Earl. John started to carve some wood away from the existing threshold to get a snug fit for the new nosing.

"May I walk on this?" Erma asked.

"Better to wait until I finish it." He saw the disappointment on her face. He stood up. "I just don't want any of the boards to split or shift." He put one foot on it gingerly. "We need it snug."

Erma smiled at him. She came to where he stood. Together they stepped on the floor. Erma's hair had come free, and it tumbled wildly around her face, concealing the shadowy pockets of her eyes and cheeks. She looked simultaneously beautiful and ghostly. She looked at him and put her arms out as if preparing to waltz. She was waiting. John could hear his heart pounding in his ears. He took a step toward her and at that moment, two headlights swung into the drive and lit up the pale skin of his own arms, reaching.

THE LAW OF GRAVITY

Ricky Borden hit Orlando early in the evening when the sky showed a ripple of colors. The city spread in front of him with Walt Disney World like the crown jewel. He wanted to feel a flicker of adventure, but he didn't. The bed of his truck was loaded with painting supplies: ladder, scaffolding, levies, brushes, scrappers, and blower, all covered by a tarp. Inside the cab, on the floor, lay a suitcase full of clothes and on top of that, a cooler with Michelobs—some full but more empty.

Ricky hadn't seen Doug since the accident. The boys had grown up together in Asheville. After high school, Doug had enlisted in the Army and Ricky had gone to work for a local contractor. When his boss laid him off for the winter months, Ricky knew exactly what he would do.

Ricky couldn't imagine Doug, who had loped along on a stocky six-foot frame, now crumbled into a wheelchair. But when he reached Doug's apartment complex and Doug opened the door, he didn't look crumbled at all. He still wore the small gold dagger on a heavy chain around his neck and his baseball cap turned not backwards, but sideways. Rolled into the sleeve of his T-shirt was a package of chewing tobacco. He sat straight up and gave Ricky his hand.

"Hey, man," Ricky said, but rather than enthusiasm, the inflection of his voice conveyed confusion and sympathy. He cast his eyes over the wheelchair. Doug wasn't wearing shoes, just thick, white athletic socks.

"Nice place," Ricky said, but it wasn't very nice. The pictures hung crooked; the linoleum curled up in the corners and a bag of newspapers waited to go outside to the recycle bin.

"It's a rat nest," Doug shrugged. "But it's on the ground floor...." His voice trailed off. He took the beer Ricky offered and gestured his friend toward the couch, where a gray tabby cat slept.

"That's Speed Demon," Doug said. "The guys in the barracks gave him to me after the accident."

Ricky nodded. They'd talked about it—the accident—on the phone. That distance made the accident seem hypothetical. Only now, seeing Doug in the wheelchair, did he think: *my friend is a paraplegic.* Doug waited for him to say something. "That was shit luck, man," Ricky finally said.

Doug held the bottle to his chest. "It was the mud. The lousy captain kept insisting I was speeding, but I wasn't doing more than forty, man. No way more than forty." He called Speed Demon, and the cat jumped into his lap.

"I don't want to go home now," he said. "Everyone would treat me like a freak. They'd remember how I was and feel sorry for me. My parents want to build a ramp on the porch, one in the can, and put a buzzer in my bedroom. I couldn't stand that. Here, people just know me this way. I can live on the disability checks. It's better. Know what I'm sayin'?"

Ricky took a long pull of beer. He kept his attention focused over Doug's head, somewhere into the next room. He decided to tell Doug what he hadn't yet told anyone else. "Doug, I got the bad blood," he said. "I found out last month." He paused, thinking of those transfusions, how routine they'd become to him, to his survival and yet, how deadly. He shrugged. "Doctor said it had to have come from blood they had before they started screening." Ricky could see fear, like sand, shifting Doug's features. "Do you still want me here?" he asked. He knew it wasn't fair to have waited this long to tell.

"Hey, man, we stick together. It's not contagious, right?"

Ricky assured him it wasn't, at least not for the way they'd be living together.

"Well," Doug said, "sounds like we're made for each other." He took out a wad of chewing tobacco, a glistening mass of brown shreds, and dropped it into the ashtray.

They both stared at it.

Finally, they began to talk about their friends. All their old buddies had married and bought houses. Several had children. They were renovating homes, planting gardens, putting down roots.

"Well, it's you and me," Doug said.

"Yeah," Ricky sighed. "Quite a pair."

The next morning, Ricky put an ad in the paper for painting jobs. Within a week he had enough jobs lined up to keep him busy. He wouldn't take any job under thirty feet and he preferred a scaffold to groundwork. He refused to wear the standard safety belts. "They're too heavy," he complained. Finally, after days of imagining Ricky falling, Doug said, "Man, under the circumstances, shouldn't you stick close to the ground?"

Ricky shrugged it off. "Free as a bird, that's me."

Doug didn't hide his half-wince of disapproval. The image of Ricky free-falling through the air like a wounded bird was too clear.

Ricky wasn't born into a family of chance takers. His father was an insurance agent in a town thirty miles from Asheville and his mother a homemaker. He was the youngest of four—the older three all girls—so he received plenty of attention, and not just that of his family. Ricky was a beautiful child—a soft light shone on his pale skin, and his eyes were wide and innocent, framed by dark, curly lashes. Those eyes and his smile, always slow and gentle, captivated strangers, who knelt to his level as if drawn to be as close as possible.

And yet, more often than not, Ricky would look away, just over his admirer's shoulder, forcing that person to turn too, to see what it was that caught his interest. But whatever it was, it was invisible. It wasn't an animal or another person or even a passing car. Ricky's family noticed this strange preoccupation with thin air, but his parents attributed his "distancing," as they termed it, to another source: hemophilia. By the time he was nine months old, he had suffered his first "bleed." Ricky spent a good part of his second year in the hospital. Every exploratory jump from the sofa or the kitchen chair or coffee table or window ledge resulted in a trip to the emergency room and usually an overnight stay to replenish his blood supply and stabilize the bleeding, which occurred underneath the skin, stretching the normally soft and alabaster tissue to a purple swollen mass.

"Ricky! Stay away from those stairs—"

"Ricky, no. You can't jump into the pool."

"Ricky—how many times have we told you? That bike is for riding in the back yard only. *On the grass.*"

By the time he was five, chance was no longer just a word to Ricky—it was a spirit that accompanied him, like his own footsteps. A spirit with a breath of its own, cold and forceful, tossing him one way, then another, like a seed with wings. He felt pushed to do things, to try things out. As he got older, the bleeds decreased, and his parents expected him to outgrow his rebellion, but without the bleeds, the risks just became more daring.

"Did you ever have the urge to just plunge, head first?" Ricky asked Doug one night. He'd had three beers and no dinner.

Doug leaned toward the stove, holding the spatula in mid-air. "You mean, just end it?"

Ricky turned away. "No. . . not like that. Just doing it so you could be totally, fuckin' free."

Doug wedged the spatula underneath the burgers, flipped them and pressed out the remaining bloody juice before he answered. "For three seconds maybe, or for however long it takes to hit the ground. Then what?"

Ricky shrugged. "I didn't say I'd ever do it. Relax man, all right?"

Doug let the conversation drop. But the next morning, after Ricky left for work, he got on the phone with the yellow pages in front of him. The first tour guide said, "Bungee? No sir, we don't arrange risk expeditions. We specialize in cruises." The second number he called the woman asked, "You want land-based or water?"

"Water," Doug said. He didn't tell her, but he was considering the odds of survival if the cords broke. "But it has to be high, or my friend won't do it."

"Okay, water and high."

Doug arranged for a private Sunday jump, when the business was usually closed. He paid an extra hundred for that and three hundred more for an unlimited number of jumps for an hour, in case Ricky wanted them.

The next day, Doug took the bus to Disney World's Magic Kingdom. Since the accident, he hadn't been out alone for more than a couple of hours at a time. The guy at the entrance gate took his money and then looked behind him.

"I don't need an escort," Doug said. "Can I have my change, please?"

The guy handed him his change and Doug passed through the gate and began making his way down Main Street, USA, stopping just once to admire the turrets and spires of Cinderella's Castle.

The first ride he tried was Space Mountain. From his position in the long circuitous line, he could see the giant Disney characters: Mickey, Pluto, Donald, stationed around the grounds, waving, shaking hands, posing for pictures with children. Snappy bands marched, playing tunes that were vaguely familiar. Doug remembered how much he'd wanted as a kid to go to Disney World with his family, but his parents couldn't afford it. But then Ricky's family went, and they took him along. He was supposed to keep an eye on Ricky, make sure he didn't do anything crazy. For five days he was Ricky's guardian. When, at the end of the five days, they all got back on the plane without having visited an emergency room at all, Ricky's father thanked him. "Douglas, you're a good boy." He pressed a small, flat box into Doug's hand. "Open it later."

When Doug opened the package that night, he found a genuine Mickey Mouse watch, with a black leather band. He'd worn that watch for years and still kept it in his socks drawer. And he never told Ricky's parents that the only way he'd been able to keep Ricky from getting hurt was to perform the daring acts himself. He stuck his arms out when he wasn't supposed to. He stood up in the Monorail and let go of the bar. All at Ricky's command.

His time to enter Space Mountain had come. The attendant was a big guy, and with the help of the person behind Doug, he got him strapped in. "Hey," Doug joked, "isn't this better than lifting weights?"

The music and lights blared and as the ride started, people screamed. Doug held on and closed his eyes. He listened to the other passengers screaming—voices rising in expectant panic and then crashing over the brink to wild delight. Suddenly he was laughing too. Every precipitous drop, each unexpected turn, he hung on.

When the ride was over, the attendant and the same fellow passenger lifted him out. He held them and slapped their backs.

"Thanks," he said. "That was pretty awesome." They were laughing too. They seemed to have forgotten their awkwardness with his paralyzed body. He went on to Big Thunder Mountain, the Jungle Cruise—there were so many rides—and he didn't stop riding until the sun had disappeared and he heard a mother yelling to her child. "Will-yum. *Get over here*. Right *now*."

The child started to cry. Snatches of music wafted on the air. Finally, he recognized the tune he'd been hearing all day—"When You Wish Upon a Star." Doug decided it was time to go home.

Ricky met a girl that same night. That morning, he had asked Doug to prepare Shake n' Bake chicken and Rice-A-Roni for dinner, but he decided to stop for a quick beer at the Robinson Crusoe Cafe. She stood at the pool table, setting up shots for the guys. Ricky sat at the bar and watched her. Her straight blond hair was swept up into a high ponytail on the back of her head, in one of those bunchy cloth-covered elastics, and every time she bent over, the long fine tail brushed the felt-covered table. She kept flicking it back with her hand. Her jeans fit snuggly and she wore a long flannel shirt over them with the sleeves cut off. He could see by her biceps and thighs she was tight. He was just finishing his beer when she slid onto the stool next to him.

"Hey," she smiled at him.

The bartender poured her a beer and put it on the counter. "This is Cindy," he said. "At least let me introduce her."

Cindy shrugged. "Get lost, Patrick. Go home to your mother."

Ricky laughed, a laugh that stayed wedged in his throat. He couldn't imagine running home to his mother now, and yet somehow he wished that he could and that she could make things better.

"You want something besides a beer?" he asked the girl.

She smiled, her jade green eyes half-closed and coy. "Strawberry daiquiri. That sounds good." So Ricky's one beer turned into two, then three. He thought about Doug sitting at the kitchen table, the low hanging lamp showing the bald spot that had started far back on his head and he knew Doug would sit there a long time, just waiting for him. His big shoulders would slump over and finally it would dawn on him: Ricky wasn't coming home for dinner. Ricky thought about it and then he put his hand on the girl's—Cindy's—thigh. "You ever done it twenty feet in the air on a scaffold?"

Her eyes opened wide for a minute, then settled back at their half lids. "I like height," she said. "But I'm not into slivers. You got a blanket?"

He paid for the drinks and drove Cindy to the building he'd been working on all week. It was late, and this block of mainly commercial buildings was deserted. Cindy leaned against the brick, her arms folded tightly under her chest so he could see the swell of her breasts tipped up and eager. She lit a cigarette while he set up the ladder to the scaffolding. "I've done some wild things," she said, blowing the smokeaway from him over her shoulder, "but this may be the best yet. Where are you from?"

"Maine," he lied. "Moosehead Lake."

"Is everybody in Maine like this?"

Ricky looked at her. "Like what?"

"No. I don't mean that in a bad way," she said. "I just wonder if they're all a little wild." He could see now that she was young. A peace sign was drawn in ink on her wrist.

"This isn't your first time, is it?" he asked.

"No," she said, and the way her face became old suddenly, her eyes and mouth weighted like anchors, he believed her. Her shirt had slipped, exposing a creamy shoulder.

"In Maine, we like high places." Ricky stepped closer and took the cigarette from her hand and flipped it onto the tar. "That way we can see the stars better." He lifted her hand to his mouth and kissed the peace sign. He could smell the soap she used. Lilacs. He hadn't been with anyone since the diagnosis. He closed her arms around his neck.

"Wait," she said. "Aren't we going up?"

He paused. The pressure, like paint dust, had settled in his lungs. He should tell her. Then he thought of Doug again, sitting at the table, waiting. No. He wouldn't tell her. He helped her up the ladder and she climbed to the top of the scaffold.

Afterwards, he could have dropped her off at her apartment, but he wasn't ready. He wanted to feel something, some relief, but if anything, the only thing he felt was the hole, that aching pit of emptiness, growing bigger. He took her home with him. Doug was in his room—asleep or awake, Ricky didn't know. The note on the table read, "*You could of called. Your plate's in the fridge.*" Ricky crumbled the paper and put it in his pocket and led the girl to his room. She kissed him more sweetly this time. He wanted to like her; he could see she was beginning to like him.

"How long are you in Florida for, Mr. Moosehead?"

Ricky plopped onto the bed and pulled her down next to him. "Don't make any plans for me, okay?"

She pulled her legs up and curled into a fetal position away from him. "Yep, that's me. Don't expect anything but a lay."

"Hey." He reached his hand under her shirt and felt her ribs, like ridges he could scale. "We got three hours. Let's sleep, okay?" They were quieter the second time. She was gone when he woke up, and he couldn't remember if she'd even told him her last name.

Doug was cooking sausages and eggs, and Ricky knew he was pissed because he kept banging the frying pan on the stove to roll the sausages, instead of turning them with a fork.

"So, did you have a good night?" Doug took the sausages off the stove and dumped them on a paper towel to soak up the fat. He kept his back to Ricky.

"Not really," Ricky said.

"Well, I hope she did," Doug said. "She may pay a high price for it."

"We all pay a price in this lousy life," Ricky said.

Doug put the eggs and sausages on a plate and balanced the plate on his lap as he turned his chair toward Ricky. "You think it's like that? Just one big punishment?"

Ricky wiped his fork with a paper napkin. "What do you think? Are you having fun in that chair?"

Doug let out a slow hiss, then he bit his lip and the hissing stopped. He threw the plate; a shower of egg and meat hit the floor. The plate hit the sink and shattered.

Ricky scrambled out of his chair to grab the cat that came running for the food. "No, Speedy," he crooned. He held her under one arm. "I'll go get the mop," he said. He came back and got down on his hands and knees to clean up the mess. When he came close to Doug's chair he looked up.

"I'm sorry, Dougy." He used the childhood name he'd always used for his friend. "I don't know what to do."

Ricky eased Doug from the truck into his wheelchair and then they moved toward the guy standing on the bungee platform. He was wearing a short-sleeved army jacket and his broad shoulders pushed at the seams of the fabric. His hair was white, his complexion clear and his face wrinkled around the eyes. A Chinese yin-yang symbol was tattooed on his forearm.

"You operating the jump?" Doug asked.

The man nodded. "It's always me," he said. "Ray Thon."

Doug stuck out his hand. "Doug Marl, and this is my friend, Rick Borden. Thanks for opening up on a Sunday."

Ray took each of their hands firmly. Ricky could feel the man's warmth radiating through his skin. He pulled his hand away, but Doug let the man hold his hand longer. "Are you planning on jumping today?" Ray asked Doug.

"We're both going," Ricky said.

Ray kept his gaze on Doug. "You really want to jump?"

"Yeah." Doug drew his hand back. "Is there something against cripplesjumping?"

"No, you can jump," Ray assured him. "I'd be glad to have you. I just asked if you wanted to jump."

"I didn't drag him along, if that's what you mean," Ricky said. "He wants the same thing I want."

"What's that?" Ray asked.

"Teach us how to stay out there." Ricky pointed to the empty chasm of space beyond the bridge.

Ray shook his head. "You boys are mixed up." He looked at Ricky as he spoke. "What you want to control isn't out there. It's in here." He tapped his head, and then he beckoned them to look over the parapet of rock that began the bridge. "This whole city. The whole entertainment industry here is built on creating a world that doesn't exist. It's cheap and fake as shit."

Ricky smirked. "So, what are you doing here then?"

Ray smiled. "I get to meet people like you."

"What's that mean?" Doug asked.

"You know," the jump-master nodded to Ricky.

"I do?" Ricky lit a cigarette, flicked the burned match behind him. "All I want to do is get out there and fly like a bird." He yanked the cigarette out of his mouth. "Can we do that or not?"

"Sure," Ray said. "We can get right to it." He went over to the gear and began to straighten out the unwieldy cord.

"Can you believe this guy?" Ricky said to Doug.

Doug shrugged. He was looking at the flexible cable, thick like an umbilical cord, but still... just a cord between him and the water below. Beads of sweat glistened on his upper lip.

"Hey, you losing your nerve?" Ricky asked.

Doug shook his head.

"Just leave him be," Ray said. "Everyone makes their own decisions up here."

Doug started wheeling himself forward. "I'm ready," he said. "I want to go first."

Ray crouched down in front of Doug. "When you get out there," he said, "I want you to keep your eyes on the other side of the bridge. Keep your eyes there and throw your arms up. Can you do it?"

Doug turned his chair so he could see where Ray was pointing. "Yeah," he said. "Up. Everything up. I can do that."

Ricky put his hand on Doug's shoulder. "I'm right behind you, man," he said. "Right behind you."

"We'll pull him up before you jump," Ray said. "You can help me get him back in his chair."

"I'm ready," Doug said to no one in particular. He kept his eye on the exact spot on the bridge where he'd jump and began pushing himself there. Ray followed. He fastened the cord around Doug's ankles, and then helped him up onto the rail of the bridge. Doug grasped the man's arms and looked back at Ricky, who gave him a thumbs-up sign. "Okay," he said. "I'm ready."

Ray nodded. "Count to three," he said. "One, two, three!" He shoved him over the side.

From thirty feet back, Ricky could see his friend's body stiffen in fear. He didn't want to, but he lost some respect for

Doug just the same. They hadn't talked about it this way, but he saw himself, he saw them together kicking Death in the teeth. He wanted to say to Death what he wouldn't be able to say later. *I'm not going with you.* But Doug was all clenched up, tight and afraid. He'd have to do it himself, do it the right way.

Ray came back toward him. "You got a loyal friend," he said. Ricky shrugged. He could see Doug bouncing up and down, up and down, each bounce less vigorous than the one before.

"You know what he's doing reminds me of the way bungee started. It was the South Seas Islanders. They tied vines to their ankles and leapt off cliffs, trying to prove their prowess to young maidens. That's what your friend just did—tried to prove himself to you."

Doug was swaying gently from side to side.

Ray turned toward the release lever.

Before Ray could pull the lever, Ricky grabbed the cord and pulled it, sending Doug snapping up and down again.

"Hey," Ray protested. "Don't do that. Get away from that railing. Let's get your friend down, and then we'll set you up to jump."

Ray took his eyes off Ricky for just a moment. Ricky took the opportunity. He kicked off his shoes and climbed onto the rail.

"Hey, man. Come on!" Without having released the cord, Ray came back to Ricky, holding his hands out like an offering. "We can't just let your friend hang there. The poor guy was petrified to jump. He did it for you. Why would you do that to him?"

Ricky spread his hands to indicate he had no idea. Why was it he had no feeling in his heart? He hadn't felt anything for that girl, or even for Doug, who he knew was scared shitless by jumping, but did it anyway. Ricky unbuttoned his shirt.

"What are you doing?" Ray asked.

"I have the HIV virus."

Ray lowered his head. "I see."

Ricky stripped off the shirt and threw it over the bridge. It floated like a kite in the wind and then twisted in a downward spiral.

Just then, Doug began to shout Ricky's name.

"Listen to him," Ray said. "He saw your shirt. He knows what you're doing."

"What's that?" Rick could barely hear his own voice. He closed his eyes. At first the breeze felt cold and he shivered, but then he could feel the sun on his skin. It was warm.

"Don't do it," Ray said.

Ricky opened his eyes and squinted. The sun was directly before him, burning and powerful. He looked away, up the wide swatch of river where some sailboats flecked the water. But his gaze was drawn back to the bungee cord just below his feet. It had stopped its wild movement, but Ricky could still hear Doug calling out his name. He marveled at the way sound rose and spread, not like the weighted body, not like that at all. He listened carefully to the syllables—"Rhhhi-kee"—balanced so beautifully on the air.

JOHN MASON'S EYE

On his eleventh birthday, John Mason received the legacy for which his parents had been preparing him his entire life, going all the way back to his birth, when his mother Hattie set his wicker basket beside her in the cannery and talked to him about their hopes and dreams, separating ripe fruit from the bruised as she talked.

When Harold came along three years after John, Hattie and Obadiah sold the fruit cannery to increase their dairy herd. Cows took more time, but paid more money. Hattie hired a neighbor girl to come in during chores to watch Harold. John was old enough then to stay at the barn with them, and they assigned him chores like scooping grain for the cows.

Obadiah would say, "You got this one, John? Let me see. How much you got there, boy? By God. Right. Now dump the scoop right in there like I taught you."

Their son's enthusiasm relieved Hattie and Obadiah. "Yes," Obadiah told Hattie. "He's the farmer."

Family farms sewed the people of Belaport together into a community, but Obadiah Mason wanted more. He wanted one of his boys to take the farm and the other he wanted to become a doctor, like his brother Asa, set up in New York. His was one of the old families, not prosperous, but smart, and he wanted each generation to progress.

So he saved. And starting when Harold was two, Obadiah said he would be the doctor. He would not let the boy milk cows or do any dangerous work—he was protecting his son's hands for the future. Surgery. And he told John, "You take a look around. All this is yours."

"All this" was a hundred acres, an average-sized farm, and seventy head of cattle, the orchard, pigs, sheep, chickens, an assortment of cats and dogs, some geese, a few rabbits. Until John's eleventh birthday.

On that day, Obadiah packed John and a picnic lunch into the wagon. He didn't tell his son where he was taking him, but John knew it was some place important, a place that dealt just with him, because when Harold started to follow them, his mother caught him by the shoulders and held him.

John heard his brother crying over being excluded as he and his father headed down the road.

"You have any idea where we're going?" Obadiah asked.

"No, sir," John said.

Obadiah smiled. The horses trotted along in silence. John followed his father's lead, nodding hello to other carriages that passed them. Finally, Obadiah turned the carriage down a long, rutted path. The horses picked their way carefully over the uneven ground. In the middle of the woods, Obadiah stopped, tied the carriage, lifted out the picnic basket, and set off through the trees, leaving John to follow.

John began to wonder if Obadiah had forgotten him when suddenly his father turned and lifted him. "How far can you see?" he asked.

"Clear over to that stone wall." John pointed to a spot a few hundred yards from where they stood.

"That's the south boundary," Obadiah said. Then he turned and pointed past John's line of vision. "North, east, west...we've just doubled the size of the farm," he said. "A hundred acres more."

"Ours?" John asked. Adding a hundred acres made their farm one of the largest in the county; even at his age, he understood the significance of that.

"Yours, really," Obadiah said. "My father did the same for me, and someday you'll do the same for your son. This is your land, John." He looked off through the trees, a softness loosening his face. Then, without another word, he laid out the beef tongue sandwiches, hard-boiled eggs, and apple pie, and they ate.

At home that night, after they ate birthday cake and sang, Obadiah described the land to his wife and youngest son.

"I'd like to build you another house there someday," he told Hattie. "A place we can live when we get old and John's taking care of us."

Harold pushed his cake away, untouched, and glared at his older brother. John looked at his father for some clue of how to act, but Obadiah seemed happy eating cake. Hattie put her arm around Harold and pulled him close. "Eat your cake," she said.

It was the next day that Harold climbed into the grain bin, a job he had been forbidden to try. He would prove to his father he was worthy. He slid the door open and poked the grain with a stick. It jammed in the chute. Harold climbed onto the ledge and jabbed again, this time with his leg. He could not quite reach. With both hands, he gripped the upper ledge and kicked again, harder. The grain fell like an avalanche, covering his legs and pulling at his torso. He couldn't hold on. Down the chute he went, his mouth, his nose, his eyes, all filling with grain. Grain pressed the last gasp of air from his lungs, leaving only fear. Luckily, Obadiah had the door of the chute open at the other end, and when Harold's heels appeared, he knew what had happened.

"Christ, boy, you could have killed yourself," he said, tugging until his son inched out like a sack of corn feed. A week's supply of grain lay on the cement floor. Obadiah scooped it into a burlap sack while Harold coughed out grain and gasped for air. He watched his father, tears forming in his eyes. That was as close as Harold got to showing Obadiah he could compete with John.

The next day, the boys resurrected from the barn loft a wooden bull's-eye and some smooth feather-tipped arrows. They rolled the target down to a secluded corner of the bottom hay field, far from their parents' sight. They had been told shooting the bow and arrow was only to be done under their parents' supervision until they were skilled enough to shoot alone. Then, they would be allowed to hunt game in the woods. John, being older, had practiced more, but it was Harold who loved the sport. It was John's idea to practice that day. He wanted to do something to ease the tensions between them.

"Harry, now remember," John yelled to his brother from where he was adjusting the board. "Plant your feet shoulder width apart and three fingers—"

But John never got any farther. Harold had already positioned his feet correctly and was fitting the arrow against the bow, testing how far back to go, when he sent it shuddering through the air. John turned just in time to hear the sharp little shoot splitting the air, its whistle so fast the sound of it paralyzed him. He felt the metal tip rip the corner of his eyelid and continue into the tender flesh of his eye. He was sure he'd been set on fire. He dropped to the ground, clutching at his face and kicking up dirt with his boots.

Whenever he thought back to the accident, he couldn't remember any sound except the whistle of the arrow. No cry of warning from Harold. No scream of pain from himself as the arrow pierced him. Only the high-pitched whistle, then a white and blinding silence that froze the moment in time, the moment until he felt his father's strong arms lift him and hug him to his chest. He remembered feeling Obadiah's heart beating hard.

John didn't remember pulling the arrow out while he lay on the ground. Or the doctor trying to stave the bleeding—profuse bleeding, which he later explained was a sign of a surface puncture, something to be thankful for. If only he hadn't gotten an infection. But he did, and then the eye specialist in New York had to take the eye out.

During those three months, John stayed with Uncle Asa and his family. The daily trips to the eye specialist left him time for thinking about the look on Harold's face before he let the arrow fly. Harold's anger had curled his mouth so that he looked like an old man, not a child. John could not erase that picture from his mind, so he changed it, feature by feature. He saw Harold's mouth gaping open with fear, not hate, and his eyes wide with shock and regret, not satisfaction. He resolved that he would forgive Harold when he got home, and he would tell his father that he must treat them equally in the future.

The doctor had done a good job fitting him with an eye that didn't recede far into the socket as some did. From across a room, a person might not even notice that he wore a false eye. Up close, it showed more, because the eye did not track or match its mate's movement, although the doctor assured him that would improve as the muscles strengthened. John worried that his family might be embarrassed, but at the train station his father greeted him easily, as if he'd just gone off to summer camp, and spent the entire ride home discussing the farm.

When they entered the house, Harold was at the table, his head bent over his arithmetic problems. John wanted to hug him and whisper, "It's okay. I know it was a mistake." But his mother ran to him first and held him close, then at arm's length and asked him one question after another—Do you feel pain? Is there medication to take? Did they take good care of you? How are Uncle Asa and the family? She ran her hand over his eye, and then it seemed that any embrace John might give his brother would only call attention to his guilt.

Obadiah stood back in the corner. "All right, Hattie," he said, finally. "That's enough. Let's get him unpacked." So his mother led him to his room—the one he and Harold had shared.

"You're a handsome boy," she whispered to him. "Your eye doesn't change that one bit."

John tried not to notice the tears in his mother's eyes. She stepped aside so that he could see his room. It was freshly painted, light yellow, with white trim and curtains, and a braided rug near his bed. Harold's bed was gone.

"We thought you boys were getting too old to share a room. We gave the study to Harold," Hattie explained.

"Oh," John said. He'd always liked sharing a room with Harold. He wished Harold had followed them from the kitchen. He didn't want a room of his own; he wanted to know if his brother still loved him or could love him in their now fractured world.

Before John could even finish unpacking, Obadiah came and summoned him for chores.

"I'm tired. I think maybe Harry will have to help you tonight." John sat on the edge of his bed.

Obadiah shook his head. "Get your barn clothes on. I won't keep you long."

John shivered. His father's voice, quick and forceful, followed a trajectory like that of the arrow determined to reach its target. John changed his clothes in a hurry. Harold did not look up from his schoolwork when they passed him in the kitchen.

Obadiah opened the door. John looked back at his brother bent over his studies.

"Be back soon, Harry," he said. Still, no response. John stepped outside, blinking, trying to force the unresponsive eye into place, trying to rectify his skewed vision.

He worked quietly at his chores, patting the cows, taking in the smells he'd missed: the hay, fresh grain, the animals' fur, all of it. Then he got his father's permission to go back to the house. Harold was still at the table with his work. John removed his boots and overalls and slid into the chair beside his brother.

"Harry?" He could hear his mother upstairs moving about.

"Please don't hold it against me." As soon as Harold said it, he felt better. Harold looked up, a sideways glance. He folded back the page of his book and closed it.

They heard their mother's footsteps on the stairs. So little time, they both knew.

"Does it hurt?" Harold asked.

"No," John spoke fervently. "No, it doesn't."

"Can I... can I see it?" Harold's voice had dropped to a whisper.

John popped the eye into the palm of his hand and offered it to his brother, leaving the socket empty and sunken.

The elliptical piece of glass, with its dark iris, stared up at them, unblinking.

"It's never going to be the same," Harold said, and John knew he didn't mean the eye. "I never wanted things to be this way between us." He gripped the prosthetic eye tight between both hands. "I keep going back over and over it. I had a good grip, John. I swear—I don't know how—"

"Harry?" John waited for his brother to open his eyes before he continued. "I can forgive anything," he said. "Just tell me the truth. Was it an accident?"

"That's the thing." Harold shook his head, clutching the eye tighter, trying to avoid his brother's gaze. "I think so. I want to say so, but I don't know, John."

John wanted to hug his brother, seeing the way Harold hunched over prosthetic eye, almost as if in penance. Seeing that was truth enough.

THE ANCESTOR'S VOICE

In the southeast corner of Connecticut, three rivers flow and meet. First, the Shetucket makes a semicircular sweep and receives the Quinebaug and then together they join the Thames, flushing water into this once wild tract of land nine miles square. Of the three, I love the Quinebaug River most, coming as it does with a rapid current through a hilly country, channeling its way around ledges, spraying foam and diving headlong over the parapet of rock, free for a moment, then caught, a reminder to me that even nature faces encumbrances.

These rivers sustained us. Fishermen constructed pens in the shallow waters of the Shetucket and then they plunged in and beat the water to drive bountiful portions of shad into captivity. But the Thames was the bigger river, called Great River by the Indians. It runs for fourteen miles—right into the Long Island Sound. Ships navigated half its length, harvesting mackerel, bass, eels, oysters, lobsters, and even sturgeon, that long bony fish with its blunt nose and coveted eggs.

But not everything yields easily here among these rivers; a constant and shadowy reminder of aggression spills like a current back to Uncas, Chief of the Mohegans. The story I remember best is the one of Uncas slaughtering his enemy,

Narragansett Chief Miantonomoh. The story goes that Uncas cut out a piece of Miantonomoh's shoulder and shook it in the air before he ate it and proclaimed it the sweetest meat he ever tasted. The murder brought the fury of the Narragansetts and other tribes upon Uncas and his Mohegans. The English protected Uncas until finally, war-weary, he and his brothers sold them nine square miles of land. For seventy pounds. Some say the English had planned all this. Some say it's not true. But everyone who heard the story heard that Uncas never raised his eyes again to the sky. I think of him, poor broken Uncas, as part of my own family, lost, also plagued by betrayal and passion for the land, forces set in motion so many hundreds of years ago.

In 1875, I came east and married Elias Brewster, the eldest of two brothers. Elias and I met through a series of correspondences he shared with his cousin, Nellie Evanstan, who was my best friend. Sometimes Elias wrote beautiful descriptions of the land and sometimes he wrote silly things, like the story of a local cobbler who claimed to see the ghost of his best friend on Crawford Ledge one moonlit night and how this young man could not steady his hands to work on another pair of shoes again, ever, although everyone in town knew it was whiskey, not ghosts, that owned him. I commented on the inventiveness of his phrasing and Nellie shared my comments with Elias. Soon we were writing directly to each other, and then his letters became more intimate, more serious. His father had died and left him the farm; he wanted a wife, and a family to run the farm. Elias proposed to me by letter, and by letter I accepted. Coming east seemed such a cultured thing to do. The east had cities and the ocean. Nellie and I copied the design for my wedding dress from a picture of the New York fashions, and we chose rich Chinese silk.

The journey took three days. The train arrived into Willimantic early one cold May morning, and as it released its steam and the air around the station house turned white, I rose from my seat and smoothed my dress. In the window, I saw my reflection. Elias would find me strong and small. Perhaps plain, my features were regular, my eyes green, but dark like wood bark, my teeth sharp and straight, my skin sallow, like lard—but I willed him to look for the spirit, that zest that gave my appearance some interest. Although I didn't believe that Elias cared for beauty, I still wanted him to desire me.

As I stepped onto the platform, he was there in front of me. His hair was the color of blanched almonds, his coarse curls touched his cheeks innocently, but his thin nose lengthened his handsome face and made him appear sad. That brooding sent a current through me, drawing me in and scaring me at the same time.

"Mary?" He did not use my full name, Mary Louise.

"Yes, it's me, Elias." I wanted him to look at me long enough so I could know what he thought of me, but my voice was so small I could barely hear it myself; it did not command attention.

"The carriage is this way." Elias turned to maneuver us through the crowd.

We traveled south to Belaport. Elias held the reins tight on the sorrel mare I came to love, called Old Eyes. The trees blinked with buds and men with their plows and horses worked the fields. Elias seemed uncomfortably shy. Each time the jostling carriage pushed us together, he shifted away, and no matter what I talked about, he couldn't seem to speak more than a few words. I wondered what had happened to the Elias I had fallen in love with, the Elias of the letters I carried in a bundle in my satchel. But as we approached Belaport, he pointed ahead. "Here," he said. "This is the Curtin's homestead. Seventy acres or so. Good land, house high on a knoll, flat fields and good drainage." I heard the poetry again and breathed, relieved until he said, "He has only daughters now. He had a son who didn't survive the winter."

As he began to talk more about the surrounding homesteads, I pondered on his meaning and the roughness of this life. When we reached the center of the city, we stopped. Clean brick buildings and shiny brass lights lined Main Street. Tall ships lined the harbor spread out below and put me at ease again.

"We can skate here in winter," Elias offered. "The harbor freezes."

"I love to skate," I said.

He seemed happy with that. He took my hand. "You'll know all this soon enough," he said. "I want to show you the farm."

During that ride, I fell in love. First with the birch trees, then every hill, even the stone walls, and then with Elias. He clearly loved it all so much.

The next day, we married. I did not meet William until after the ceremony. I knew of the rift between the two brothers. Elias had told me in a letter that when their father gave him the homestead, he also bought William a smaller piece of land on the outskirts of town to "even things out." The boys' mother had gone to live with William; she had apparently always favored him.

But those problems surfaced later. During the wedding, the family was gracious to me and William especially welcomed me. "You'll be good for us, I think," he said. After the wedding guests left, Elias did the most surprising thing for the man I was expecting him to be: all practicality. He sat down at the piano and played. First, a whimsical little piece, I don't remember what, then he turned and looked at me and his eyes lost their grimness, and he played something deeper, stronger. He leaned his shoulders into the keys, and I imagined him leaning that way over me. I put my hand on his shoulder and led him to our bed, the first of many times that spring, each time more hungry and curious, but also more purposeful. Soon we knew: I was going to have a child.

At night, he came in from the fields happy. He played music for me, or I read to him while he carved a cradle, then a small bureau. We waited together.

My labor started during a snowstorm and Elias went for Grace Pembrote. I had waited too long, and by the time Elias set out, my contractions nearly knocked me off my feet. Before the next one could strike, I carried the bowl of hot water to the nightstand, along with clean rags and a knife to cut the umbilical cord. I took deep breaths and talked to her—I knew it was a girl, I could feel her as such, could almost see her as she pushed her way like a ball of fire through the birth canal. I was singing and screaming as her head crowned and I saw in the bureau mirror her head appear into this world. I doubled over in pain and effort to see the shoulders emerge and with a final push and rip of flesh, she lay there between my legs, an infant whole. I picked her up and held her to my chest, then I cleaned as much as I could, wrapped her in a clean blanket, and waited. I worried perhaps Elias would be disappointed that the first child was a girl, but if so, he did not show it, but seemed only relieved that we had both survived the ordeal. Before he could ask the question, I said, "I'd like to name her Hannah, for your mother."

Each day blurred into the next, so many hours without sleep. Elias paced the floors.

"Why doesn't she stop crying?" he asked. My milk had come in, but I couldn't get Hannah to drink. I developed a fever as well. Grace Pembroke had tried to clear the phlegm from Hannah's nose, but it had traveled to her lungs and she was struggling to breath.

"You're burning up," Elias said. The few hours he slept, he slept on the kitchen floor, near the woodstove. "There's something wrong with her," he said finally, staring into the crib, and his tone was flat.

On the fourth day of the storm, Elias took her when I left the bed to get wood. He took her in a basket and I saw him crossing the field, the river a dark ribbon just ahead of him, and I ran, my legs sinking like rods in the snow.

"Elias!" I called. When I finally reached him, I had no breath. I grabbed for the basket.

"She's suffering, Mary Louise."

He would not let go the basket. I reached inside and scooped her up. The baby did not cry as I tucked her under my coat and hurried back to the house. The next morning, she died.

The next child was a boy, Elias Jr., and the three that followed were also boys: William, John, and Daniel.

One spring day, Elias needed to ride to Asheville to buy lumber for an addition to the barn. I went along to see the countryside. I expected that in such a small state, this area would look much like Belaport, but as we moved north, the landscape changed. The roads narrowed to rocky paths. Thick woods crept right up and branches reached out like impatient hands, ready to slap and scratch us if we moved over to let another carriage by. There weren't many. This land was sparsely settled. The air smelled sharp of pine and something less tangible—disappointment, perhaps.

But the thing that disturbed me most was the darkness. Even though it was a sunny day, the trees shrouded the light. In Belaport, the Atlantic Ocean was a vast mirror refracting the brilliant sunlight for miles.

"Just a few more miles to the sawmill," Elias said.

I nodded.

"Are you alright?" Elias asked.

I was expecting our fifth child. "I'm fine." I realized my voice was just a whisper.

"We don't need to go on," Elias said. "I could come back another day."

"No, keep going." I could hear the Quinebaug River rushing off. We neared the sawmill, and the sound of the current was drowned out by the whine of the blade splitting logs. We rounded the bend and saw an open field dotted with piles of split logs. The smell of the hot saw and dust stung my nose. The men bent their strong bodies to hauling wood. As we made our way closer, I saw some men were missing fingers or limbs, and others stooped so they looked like deformed branches.

I gasped. "How awful," I said.

"What?" Elias asked.

"Don't you see the violence of it?"

He cocked his head and considered. "I suppose," he said finally. Then he jumped down and went off to do his business.

After Hannah died, I took long walks. Once, I found a robin's nest with two eggs; one had hatched but the other had not. The mother hovered uneasily over me, keeping watch. She swooped back to the broken egg, the way I went to Hannah's grave. I kept the tiny plot clear. Her death seemed so unreal, so impossible.

The day I packed her dresses, Elias came in for lunch with a bunch of wild lilies. He saw the pile of clothes on the table and he looked away. The three older boys played at my feet. The two youngest were sleeping.

"I hear Abigail Tolman had a baby girl this week. Faith Leffingwell told me so."

Elias nodded.

"I thought I'd take her these things."

Again, he nodded, and touched the lilies lightly and said, "I would not have chosen it to happen. I know not what to do but see the cycle of nature in all of it, Mary Louise."

"Then take your nature," I said, handing the lilies back to him. "It is too cruel."

His eyes showed his pain, but he was a proud man. He took the flowers and went back to the fields. After that, it was to them he gave his gave his grief and love.

I took Abigail Tolman everything but a pair of white lace booties. I kept those. I kept them because the senses hunger to remember what's been lost. A smell, a touch, a sound, can bring it all back.

The boys never knew of Hannah. Elias would not allow me to tell them. Our grief was kept between us; perhaps we were ill equipped to share it. But the weight of not speaking drew her memory closer. And I visited her grave. For me, kneeling on that sunken ground, feeling the moss give beneath my weight, softened the grief. Her tiny stone read, "God gave. He took. He will restore. He doeth all things well." I went from hating those words to reciting them and later, hoping in them. Maybe they hold empty promises, but there's no shame in hoping, or remembering.

I watched Elias take up the fight with his brother. Like waking and sleeping, they fought every day, William bitter against Elias. Both caught: to obey or to reject the father's desire to run the farm. And they did. The land remained the center of everything. They argued about the best way to get the work done. The fights divided them more and more as the herd grew and Elias refused to hire help. "We can spend our profit to make the work easier or we can use it to buy more land."

"I say we pasture the herd down to the river this spring then," William insisted. "We have that fresh water supply, and we don't use it. It would save us hours of hauling water."

Elias shook his head. "No. We got to keep better watch on them than that. If we don't haul water, we won't see them every day. How can we keep track of the cattle like that? We can't."

William saw me at the window. He lowered his voice and said something I couldn't hear. But whatever it was made Elias change his mind. He agreed to pasture. Together, they built the fence and let the herd go. For two weeks, the cattle thrived, and they saved so much time by not hauling water. They got the planting done early. Then, one day a neighbor came and said the herd was down. The cows had got some velvetleaf. They all died.

Elias exploded. "You and your shortcuts." He jabbed William in the chest. "Goddamn! Why did I listen? Why-did-I-listen-to-you?" With each word, he was pushing William.

William retreated. He was not a coward, but he would not hit Elias. Elias followed him, insisting he replace the cows with his own money. And I don't know why, but William did it. He could have just quit the whole thing, and I don't understand why he didn't.

As for Elias, I knew he would never quit. I saw the look when he touched the wet earth each spring. It was desire I saw on his face. He sniffed the ground as if it were fertile. Desire tormented him. Like blood sap in his veins. Like ice burning a gorge.

So many times, I watched William go to the willow tree that stood on the farm. I began to think of him as a willow tree, the slow whipping of the branches, bending, bending, bowing to the ground, but never breaking.

He hid behind its curtain. Once in the spring, I took my basket and, pretending to collect the flowers that grew nearby, I went to find out just what he did beneath the veil of that tree.

The dew on the branch wet my face and hands as I peered through the opening and saw William, seated on a large rock curved so he could fit in its hollow. His back was to me. His hands brushed over the stone as if he were sweeping away leaves or dirt, then he bent over his lap, scribbling and shuffling through loose sheets of paper the way a hen checks her eggs: possessively. I believe he was writing poetry. His lips moved in their own silent rhythm, and then he stopped and scribbled a word or phrase.

I did not stay. I hurriedly picked black-eyed Susans, daisies, and tiger lilies and went back to arrange them in a vase on my desk. I, too, desired some beauty in our lives. An hour later, William emerged, empty-handed. I wondered where he hid the book, but I never looked. I never did, because I know that book was filled with his dreams and his hurt. His father had given him land and cattle and a curse, but when he wrote in that book, was he free? Through the months and years, he became quieter and angrier. Then one day, it was winter. I looked out and the willow branches were like so many starving ribs and there was William, chopping down the tree. He hacked at it over and over and he chopped the trunk into cords and carted it away.

Elias went into a rage when he came home and saw the stump. He'd been off helping a neighbor build a barn, but I lied and told him I asked William to take the tree down so I could see more of the fields. It took William a long time to clear the branches, but still he was unhappy. Chopping down the tree only made things worse.

And for so long, I wondered—why didn't he leave? He could have sold his stake in the land to Elias and had enough money to do many other things. He could have been free. But instead he kept himself tied to the land, and all because of his father's dictate that they run it together.

As a young girl, I knew nothing of this land. I dreamed of changing my life, finding some adventure—whatever that adventure might be. My father loved to carve whales, and I always thought that carving whales was an odd thing for him to do since we lived in a land-locked state. He had been raised in the house I was born in, and he never left the state of Nebraska. The ocean intrigued him though, and he read many books about it.

"Oh, Mary Louise!" My mother would utter my name with some pride as well as exasperation when I told her I intended to go beyond the boundaries of our property. It wasn't much of a property. It never stirred my blood or my imagination. The lawn was flat, and the house was small with a tiny porch and a narrow staircase leading from the front hall to the upstairs bedrooms. We didn't have need for land—my father was a clerk. From our windows, we could see for miles the texture of sameness. And this I can say for my life with Elias, my life in New England: I never felt the bland pulse of monotony. This land yields its variety like a skilled lover. My desire for change, the changes I chose, brought tremendous pain, but also joy. Both forces shaped me, and in both pain and joy I was free.

I came across the plains and never went back to visit my mother but once, after my father died. Elias would not let me take all the children. He kept the older boys with him. I knew what he was thinking. Perhaps I wouldn't come back. But by that time, I was a different woman than the one who'd left Nebraska. For better or for worse, I would have come back.

The train stopped in Omaha and, when I saw my mother waiting on that platform, I just about couldn't stand. Her generous body, her good kind face. My own limbs felt heavy as water. I wanted to cry in her arms, but my grief had moved me to a place so far from her. To bring that grief home for her to worry over when she had her own seemed wrong. I took the boys, one in each hand, and I walked down that stairway, smiling.

That week, I helped my mother pack my father's things, and we found a letter Elias had written him before we were married, promising to take good care of me.

"Has he treated you good?" my mother asked. Her fingers plucked at a few stray threads in one of the shirts she was folding.

"Elias is the hardest worker of all the farmers." I turned away as I spoke. "If he thought there was something else I needed, he'd work even harder. Every week, I get a good allowance for supplies, and money to get the boys ice cream and buy something for myself."

She didn't say anything. I'm sure she knew and was trying to leave me some pride. But either way, I'd made the choice not to tell her. For, in truth, I did not understand myself the hardness between us. At the end of the week, I came home, and Elias was glad to see me. The next day, I walked to Hannah's grave. The three rivers, their jagged bluffs, and wooded enclaves helped heal me. The sunsets marked my daughter's death, the midnight skies my dream of holding her again. I watched so many times this land push seeds forward to life and absorb a body at death, taking back every inch, healing, healing. I walked at night where a thousand luminous stars watched and kept me and the moon committed all to memory.

I watched the seasons change. The farm boundaries changed as families prospered and moved on to trades and professions. But our land yielded crops each season. We fertilized and harrowed and planted and paced and fenced and tended. And I walked each summer through the rows of corn, letting their burnt-oat colored tassels shed their seeds on me, covering my skin with that fiber. Oh, how I loved that. I took the children walking too. Often, they played hide and seek. I could hear them rustling the strong stalks as they ran, their giggles part of the abundant bounty.

One day, Elias' mother walked with us, before she became so frail. "You children, come." She had a way of talking so that she only needed to say things once, and I'm not sure why her own sons could not manage to heed her.

The children listened. Her face, tough with all its wrinkles, opened out to them."Do you want me to show you how we make crowns?"

They nodded, all my boys. The sun lit their skin like tender eggshells.

"Each of you get me tassels from three stalks and two ears of corn. We need the silk." The children dispersed, and then Hannah spread her legs and lowered herself on the bare ground, like an old hen. I sat beside her.

"They'll bend the stalks," I said. Elias was always warning the children he'd beat them if they played in the corn.

Hannah shook her head. "No. I did this for him and William, too. He won't have a thing to say against it." The children returned with tassels and corn. Hannah commanded each of them to peel the ears and hand her the silk. She wove the tassels together, braiding three separate strands into tight rows, and then she measured each child's head and wove a crown to fit.

"Hold hands," she said, and she touched a corn stalk lightly to their shoulders. "I crown you princes of the corn." The boys smiled shyly. "And as princes, you must now have a mission. Care for this land. Reap its harvest. But boys," she leaned into their sweaty midst and wrapped her gnarled hands around their arms. "First and foremost, guard each other." The boys smiled and touched their crowns. They were happy. I knew what Hannah desired. It was the same peace I wanted. I loved them the way the morning sounds love the air: every cricket chirping, every bird calling, every leaf rustling against the wind.

Many years ago, I held Hannah, my poor feverish baby as she writhed in pain. I soaked cotton strips in cool water and wiped her burning skin, the little joints stiff and tense in my hands. I knew I would lose her and I thought, *How does a mother carry her baby in her womb, feel the tiny limbs thrash in first motion, know that the baby is testing its own strength, its own limits, the kindness of the world?* How does a mother hold all that, and then become strong enough to hold those same limbs, dead?

I did it. But I cannot tell you how, except perhaps I always hoped that what seemed like the end was not really the end. I did not expect to see or hold her in the flesh again, but I expected… something. The boys came along. I looked for it: this mysterious thing I expected in each of them, but I could not find it.

One night, months after Hannah crowned the boys, the Grange members held a harbor ice skating party and Elias and I went. We had never been ice-skating, despite Elias' promise to me that first day I arrived in Belaport. The day before the party, Elias took me to town and bought me skates.

The night of the party was a full moon. The cold air made everything crisp, and the ice was like glass—when I stepped out on the harbor, I pushed off with my legs and one glide moved me effortlessly ahead of Elias. I felt separated from all the others—I was free. I moved further out, away from them, and let my arms steer me, one way, then another, free, free. I whispered the word to myself and felt the air leave my body—free—leaving it light. I knew Elias and the others were watching, but I did not care. I could not stop myself. Later, on the way home we were quiet with each other, leaving me room to wonder at my actions. The clomping of the horse's hooves echoed on the air and we came up over the hill. Every tree seemed alive and watching. Every detail of the farm was sharp and clear in my mind and I knew that whatever disappointment I had in Elias, that our common love for this place, for the land, was a bond we had chosen, like the commitment one makes to God or a lover, and I reached across the seat and took his hand.

"Do you want to stop at the cemetery?" he asked.

I nodded.

He pulled up to the gate and came around to help me out of the carriage. He kept his arm around my waist as we walked side by side to the gate. It creaked. We both hesitated; we had not been to Hannah's grave together since the day we buried her. I sensed he was waiting for my permission. I took his hand and led him to the tiny marker. The air was still, and we stood in the silence, staring at that small piece of stone. Elias sank to his knees and brushed the snow from it so that the words were visible, then he remained kneeling.

"Elias, that night, when you took Hannah in her basket... Why?"

He looked up at me as if he had been sprung from a trap. "I was afraid her suffering was going to kill you, too. You were the one thing I could not lose. And yet, you never forgave me."

He bent over her tiny grave.

"I forgive you, Elias," I said as I put my hand on his head and thought about how my life might have turned out differently. How I might never have come east, might never have agreed to marry him, then would never have borne Hannah and buried her and borne five sons, too.

But this was my life, moving along its own course, one I had chosen and accepted and lived. I felt strong, and that strength was myself joined with the land, and it was a strength I could not and would not relinquish, no matter how it changed me, no matter how it changed.

Let me tell you what I see now. I see a man, his ear to the ground, weeping. His tears turn to silver, and melt everything on the earth. His back heaves, great wracking waves of grief make him swell like an ocean. His tears never end. His grief is for what cannot be regained. He pounds the earth with his fists. What he wants is to feel the pulse of the land. He wants the singing pulse to stir again.

THE PAINTED LADY

The Painted Lady and I grew up together. Before I gave up on reading and the schools gave up on me, when I was desperate to hold a book like every other kid, I read comic books. At first, it was just a relief to have something with pictures on the page to help me figure out the story, but then I got into them. All that action. Good versus evil. Heroes and heroines. The Painted Lady started as a comic book character, a beautiful girl but with the barest outline of humanity. A souped-up version of Barbie, she was all the comic book heroines wrapped into one. In my old sketchpads, going back to when I was eight years old, she wore clothes like Robin Hood or Peter Pan, and her most distinctive feature was her clenched fists, always swinging at the bad guys. Then we moved into what I call the Mouth Phase, when she spoke into a bubble, giving everyone lip. Man, she was pissed at what, in my drawings, I labeled the Asshole Authorities of the World (AATW.) That lasted for several years. When we hit the early teens, though, the enemy disappeared, and it was just her and me. Okay, I'll admit we had the Sex Object Phase, with headlights the size of Jupiter, but that didn't last long either, because by the time

I was seventeen, she had matured too. There was a certain expression on her face. My mother had breast cancer by then. Every day, at least once a day, I drew my Painted Lady. Suffering showed in the lines I added to her face, lines that revealed her depth, her very essence.

That was the Painted Lady I was drawing one day in my sketchpad when Nemo came into the back room of our shop in Belaport and said to me, "Willie, I got something for you. One golden Hostess cupcake, ready to go." He held the curtain open just a little so I could get a good look at her.

"Pretty nice, eh?" he said. "Maybe you should pay me for the privilege."

"Right. Two inches, Nemo." That's what I always told my girlfriend, Cheryl. It means I only see two inches at a time while I'm working, and it's just not sexual.

"Two inches, my ass," said Nemo. He flipped the curtain back, exposing us to the girl.

I stared.

She smiled like she was used to that and pointed to the sandwich board advertising the hours. It was thirty minutes to closing. "Can I still get a tattoo?"

I nodded, not quite up to words yet.

This girl dressed like a woman; I asked to see her license. Indeed, she was just eighteen. I asked her if she wanted to look at the flash. She shook her head. "I know what I want," she said. "I want the name of the guy I love, and I want you to put it right here." She pointed to a very private part.

Nemo whistled.

"Sorry." I stood behind the counter. "I don't do genitalia." It's an agreement I made with Cheryl, and it suited me fine.

The girl gave me a cold stare. "What about here?" She pointed with her thin finger to her chest.

"That's fine," I said, pushing a sheet of lettering samples in front of her. "Here are a few choices, or we can create something different."

"I want something simple," she said, choosing the first one on the list. "You won't need to draw it out first."

I frowned. I didn't like someone rushing or dictating my art. "There's a minimum charge. Ninety dollars, up front."

She fished a leather change purse out of her canvas bag and unrolled five twenties and handed them to me. "Keep the change," she said.

I handed Nemo all but the last twenty. "You can go on into the back room."

She swished around the counter and into the back.

"Have fun," Nemo whispered.

"Two inches," I reminded him. When I got into the back room, the girl handed me a piece of paper. *Eddie Fratano*. That was his name. She told me in a whisper that she was so in love with him. Walking into the small room and taking off her shirt seemed to change her. She had a towel wrapped around her, covering all but her upper chest and shoulders. I drew out the name on a sheet of paper even though she had said not to.

"Looks good," she said. "But can you make the 'o' a heart?" So I started, and she watched my hand, like she was afraid I was going to slip, which of course I didn't. When I was almost done, she blurted out, "I'm so crazy about him, and it's funny—I don't think he even knows I exist." At this point, the E-D-D-I-E F-R- was already on her chest.

"You mean—?" I held the needle away from her skin.

"Yeah." She looked down at her skin as if this guy might materialize into everything she wanted just because she carved his name on her chest. "Please finish. I'm getting cold."

"Just a minute," I said. I went to the front where Nemo was sweeping up. "Nemo, she's got me carving some guy's name, and this guy doesn't even know she exists."

"What's his name?" Nemo asked.

"Who cares, Nemo? I don't want to carve her. It's wrong."

Nemo's face got tight and he gripped the broom. "Willie, don't you start that shit. You don't get to make that decision for the customer. Go finish what you started."

"But—"

"Go finish." He pointed to the back room. "Now."

I went back and finished in a hurry. Then I sent her away through the back door. It was one of those hot days in June when even the flies couldn't move. Her high round hips swung side to side, making her little miniskirt with the lace bottom flutter. I wondered for a minute how Eddie Fratano could resist her. I went back in and started cleaning up. I could hear Nemo in the front talking to a customer, one of the regulars, a guy with half his body covered with tattoos. In the two years I had worked there, I had designed three abstract drawings for Nemo to tattoo on this guy. Right then, I saw very clearly something I had known before in a vague way: Nemo was a scratcher, and as long as I worked for him, I'd have to be a scratcher too. I told myself then and there that no matter what Nemo said, I was never going to carve a girl like that again, one who didn't have the love of the man she wanted. I shouted to Nemo that I was leaving, and then I slipped out the back door.

I drove the two blocks to the bank, where Cheryl worked as a teller. We had been together since the beginning of high school. She was waiting at the corner, wearing perfect white sneakers, with her pumps in a bag and her small purse under her arm. Her long brown hair shone, and she looked all aglow in a yellow suit. Every time I saw her, a little zap of desire went through me. She put her skinny electric body in the car and leaned over to kiss me in a whoosh of floral perfume and her own body smell, which was a hell of a lot more interesting.

"You're in a bad mood," she said.

I told her about the girl and Nemo's making me finish carving her. Cheryl frowned and checked her makeup in the rearview mirror.

"Well, what do you expect, Willie? Look what you've chosen for a profession."

"There's nothing wrong with the profession. It's who I work for." Although neither of us said anything more, Cheryl's comment bothered me. When we were in high school, my art was a turn on, but lately I was beginning to wonder.

It was Friday night, and we were meeting some friends for drinks. When we got there, Cheryl abandoned me at the door to go talk to our friends, who she saw every day anyway. As I walked by myself, I felt a little tap on my arm—my high school guidance counselor, Miss Wainwright. I gave a stiff nod and tried to slip by, but Miss Wainwright stood right up and hugged me.

"William Mann!"

"Miss Wainwright."

"Look at you." She turned my elbow so I was facing a table of teachers, who seemed like they didn't want to be disturbed.

"It's good to see you," she said. A shadow crossed her face. "Your mother? How is she?"

"She died, Miss Wainwright. About a year after we graduated."

Miss Wainwright got very serious, right into her counselor's mode. "That's very hard, Willie. I'm so sorry." She lowered her voice and put herself between me and the others at the table. I remembered her using that tone of voice with me, years ago, junior year. The SAT scores had just come in, and we were all to have conferences with our guidance counselor to identify our future goals. My SAT scores were sitting on her desk when I walked into her office. I started talking about art, and how maybe I could be an artist. I still remember the look on her face, one of physical pain. She pulled out the scores and read them silently, then looked up at me.

"Maybe you could pursue art as a hobby, but just not count on it as your professional future. Or, you could try to work up to it."

Now I said, "Miss Wainwright. I finally found a job using my artistic talent."

"You did, Willie?" she squealed in a plastic voice. "I'm so proud of you. Tell me."

"I'm a tattoo artist."

Miss Wainwright blinked, and then even though she tried to keep her smile plastered across her face, it was just too much for her. The smile fell hard. "Well, I'm happy for you, Willie." Then, she plunked herself down in her seat and went back to drinking. When I walked away, I imagined giving her a tattoo on her tight, stringy ass. I would swab her skin clean, then start with a double pack of needles and adjust the contact screw to really make the needle jump through her epidermis as I drew a bee with a gigantic stinger. Then, I would invite her to take a look, and I would say, "Now you know how much you've always meant to me: a giant pain in the ass." For the entire meal, I tried to wipe Miss Wainwright and her effect away. Cheryl laughed and joked with our friends like I wasn't there. Miss Wainwright was gone by the time we left.

"You didn't say two words tonight," Cheryl said when we got in the car.

I just shrugged, and neither of us spoke on the way back to my house. What I couldn't put in words, I tried to communicate in performance. Cheryl must have understood some of it, because when we were through she patted my chest and whispered, "It's all right, Willie," over and over, until she fell asleep.

I couldn't sleep, so I got up and left her all curled up with the blankets and went for a ride on my motorcycle. The bike helped clear my head. I stopped on the bluff overlooking the marina.

The entire harbor had been renovated with money donated by the Mohegan and Pequot tribes. The tribes ran tour boats from the harbor for casino guests. High speed ferries brought visitors from New York. New restaurants, souvenir shops, a Salvation Army store, a book store, bait and tackle shop, even our tattoo shop was doing better. Everyone in Belaport gathered there now, the way they had in the old days, according to my mother, in the summer to hang out on boats in the harbor, and in the winter to skate. My mother had loved to skate there when I was a kid. I closed my eyes and I could almost see us back there, circling, flying over the ice. I wished I had my sketchpad with me. I wanted to draw it, what I saw and felt. I wanted Nemo to feel it too. When I first met him, he was a big, bald man with a salt and pepper beard, who could bench press two hundred fifty pounds easy, but now he had esophageal cancer and spoke by burping air up through a machine in his throat. I was watching him waste away, just like my mother.

That Monday when I opened up the shop, the air itself smelled disappointed. Mondays were our slowest day, and I sat there for hours drawing. Miss Pain-in-the-Ass Wainwright and my problem with carving that girl started a streak that lasted all week. Not that we never had a slow week before, but I never thought about it in terms of a bigger picture because sooner or later, business always picked up and my needs were few as my mother used to say when she was trying not to feel guilty for being too sick to meet them. By Wednesday, I still had no customers. That evening, Cheryl and I were watching TV and I started going through my sketchpads, looking for some new flash for the shop.

Cheryl stopped my flip of the pages with her manicured finger and regarded one of my Painted Lady sketches. "Here she is," she said. "Your mother as a comic book character."

"What?" I pulled away from her.

"Absolutely. Those piercing blue eyes, your mother's dark hair. Before the chemo, she was beautiful."

"I know that," I frowned, "but the Painted Lady—I've been drawing her since I was a kid. You think this is like some Freud thing?"

Cheryl laughed a deep-throated laugh, the kind of laugh I hadn't heard from her in a long time. "Oh, Willie. Relax."

Neither of us wanted to ruin that moment. I wanted to hold on to it forever. "Will you move in with me?" I asked.

Cheryl regarded me. "Are you messing with me?"

"I'm totally serious," I said. "I want to make a bigger commitment to each other."

"And then what?" She pulled her shirt down over her irresistible belly.

"And then… maybe the next step? We get married, I guess. I don't know."

Cheryl got up and kissed me on the top of the head. "I don't think so, Willie. Come back and ask me again when you do know." I tried to pull her down, but she resisted.

"I'm going to sleep at my place tonight," she said. "You need to get a plan, Willie."

I watched her walk out the door, and I was proud of her for putting me in my place. She deserved more. I would have to do better.

The next day, there were only two customers for me, so I went into the back room, got out my private drawing pad, a fresh pack of needles, the paints, and everything else I needed to cross the threshold to artistic maturity. Once, Nemo had offered to tattoo me, and I explained I was saving my skin for my own tattoo, something special. He had reached for a pile of his kid's Legos and said, "Willie, creating a tattoo is like building something with Legos. Every skill is just like one of those Lego bricks." He looked funny with a Lego in his hand. "Lining, coloring, shading. First, we get the skills. Then, after you get them, you work one at a time and put them together." Nemo's advice had made me a professional. Some tattoo artists get their practice on fruit, then work their way up to paper plates. But really the only way to tattoo is on human skin, because there's nothing else like it. Any fruit or vegetable, the skin is too thick. A paper plate? You just go through. Nemo let me do all the lining right from the beginning. And no customer of mine ever got an infection. I was ready for this.

Drawing the Painted Lady on paper felt more right than ever before. I took my time, closing my eyes every once in a while so I could see in my mind's eye her character, not just her shape. When I was satisfied, I took the drawing over to the transposer, ran it through to get the reverse image, and then made sure everything I needed was within reach of the chair. I took off my jeans, sat down, and flipped the leg rest up. Carefully, I applied the Painted Lady's outline to my leg. Her head started on the outside of my upper thigh and her feet just grazed my knee. I gripped the outliner and began etching the thick hold line into my skin, working two inches at a time, just like always, so that, even though it was my leg and upside down at that, I saw only the lines in segments that curved, until she was all there. I filled her in with color, red and purple for her outfit, black for her hair, vibrant blue for her eyes. She stood, at home and full of attitude. When I was finishing up, Nemo came in.

"I wondered what the hell you were doing back here." He leaned over me to get a better look. "She's a beauty, Willie. You going to add her to the flash?"

I looked up at Nemo standing there with his red bandana covering the hole in his throat and the truth hit me.

"No, man," I said. "I've been thinking, Nemo. It's time I went out on my own."

Nemo let the curtain drop behind him. "What do you mean—go out on your own? I invested all this time training you. You're just starting to pay off."

"Nemo, don't pull that crap. I carried my weight from the start and you know it."

He pointed to his throat. "You see the unexpected things that can happen, Willie."

"I know, Nemo. I took care of my mother right to the end, remember?"

He nodded and looked away. He leaned against the wall and regarded me. "Well, what do you want? More money? More clients?"

I dabbed at my leg, trying to absorb the last bit of excess paint. The Painted Lady reached up my thigh like a pillar.

"I want to take my art to the next level, Nemo."

Nemo regarded me with that fatherly look I saw him give his own kid. "Willie, you're a dreamer."

That Saturday, I convinced Cheryl to take a ride to Hartford with me. We parked near the train station and immediately I vetoed that section of town. Yeah, they had a couple of good restaurants, but nobody was going to say, "Damn fine steak, now let's go get tattooed." And the train station itself would bring some riff raff I didn't want at my door. Drunks and prostitutes give tattoo artists a bad name, and we're already persecuted enough. The civic center was out, rent way too high. The neighborhoods I decided against because I wanted to be right downtown. If I was moving to the city, I wanted to feel like I was in the city. I found the shop on a quaint little street, just a few blocks south of the civic center next to a tux shop and a lingerie shop with some pretty complicated contraptions that Cheryl said would take five years to get in and out of. Did I want to see? I said hell yes.

I took down the phone number listed on the poster. On the way back home, I asked Cheryl again to move in with me. "Let's have a six-month run," I said. "And then if you can stand me, I'll give you a ring and we'll set a date."

"Is this really what you want?" She was zipping her heart locket back and forth on its chain.

"Yes." I started to tell her how I saw the future, and I was so busy making sure she knew I didn't doubt myself, I forgot to ask her if it was what she wanted. We went back to my house and made sweet mid-afternoon love. It wasn't until we were lying quiet in each other's arms that Cheryl noticed the tattoo.

"Jesus, Willie!" She rolled away from me and sat up, frowning at the tattoo. "Do you think it's big enough?"

I laughed, until I saw she was upset.

"Why didn't you tell me you were going to do this?"

"Why? Don't you like it?"

"I like it on paper, but Jesus, Willie!"

"Is this about the mother thing again? Because if it is, I think you were off base."

Cheryl took a deep breath. "Okay, Willie! You tell me. Why is this cartoon woman on your leg?"

I looked down at the Painted Lady. "This is no cartoon, Cheryl. She's like my soul expressed on the outside, where people can see."

Cheryl put her tiny hands on my face. "Nemo was right about one thing, Willie. You really are a dreamer." But her anger was gone, and I was glad.

The next day, Cheryl moved in, and I called my doctor friend, the one who was responsible for keeping Nemo's shop certified, and he called a friend in the state health department and learned there was no ordinance against tattoo shops in the city of Hartford. We were home free. The certification process was underway. So then I called the landlord, who told me the place had been empty for three months. The rent was high, but still I asked to see the shop. I saw it and fell in love. Miss Wainwright's lack of faith, Nemo's doubts, Cheryl's unspoken desire for a solid foundation—none of those things stopped me from signing the papers. In fact, they encouraged me.

The Painted Lady opened a month later after a bazillion coats of paint and a new shop window, done by Connecticut's best, with the best acrylic paints money could buy. I bought a sheet cake from Better Value and got a picture of the Painted Lady scanned onto the cake for opening day. I sent invitation cards to my customers, again with the Painted Lady's image, to come and bring a friend. They showed up. Everyone asked about her—a few of my cruder customers made comments about her while eating the cake, but most people seemed to understand the significance of this move and what it meant to me. Cheryl even managed to look cheerful, although she had cautioned me that opening my own business would be hard.

"I see all these small business owners come into the bank," she said. "Most of them fail in the first year."

"I don't plan to fail," I replied.

"You have to look at the bottom line, Willie," she said doubtfully, but still she went around serving people punch. I kept looking at the door, waiting for Nemo, hoping he would come and give me his blessings, but he didn't.

Cheryl helped me pick out some curtains, and I barely had time to hang them Monday morning before clients started coming in. Everything went fine the first week. I brought home double what I was bringing home at Nemo's and, yeah, as Cheryl pointed out, the rent was double, but still, I was just establishing myself here. A couple more weeks came and went. Then one day, Cheryl came in as I was just finishing up an enormous heart on the bicep of a Puerto Rican guy named Jimmy. The heart, one of my own drawings, had roots trailing down Jimmy's arm and a thorn stabbing its mid-section. In the thorn I drew the name of Jimmy's wife, Brenda. They had been married twenty years, and he wanted to surprise her. I went over some tips with Jimmy on how to care for his new tattoo, then he left, and Cheryl waved a piece of paper at me.

"Nemo came into the bank today, and he asked me to give this to you."

The paper was an advertisement for a tattoo art show. I remembered hearing Nemo and some other guys talk about these shows, where tattoo artists could buy their stock of flash from other tattoo artists. The ad said the flash brought ten dollars a sheet, and there would be a contest. First prize was five thousand dollars. I decided right then and there to enter the Painted Lady in the contest. When I thought of all my original flash, I thought I could pull down a thousand easily. I told Cheryl how this would help me cover the month's rent. She looked from me to the new curtains, she said, "That's great, Willie, but what about next month?"

"Maybe I'll win the contest."

"And if not?"

"I'll just keep drawing," I said.

"Willie," she sighed. "You are not looking at the bottom line. We can't go on like this forever."

One afternoon not long after that, two ladies arrived at the shop. One of them had a real Spanish accent. I learned later she was from Colombia. The other one, her friend, was local, and it was her idea to come. They were both wearing jeans and jean jackets, but those didn't look like their regular clothes. You get a feel for that in this business. I could tell by their haircuts, both stylish and careful, and their shoes. I invited them into the shop and they giggled like teenagers. One prodded the other. Finally, the one named Barbara said, "You have to forgive us. We're laughing so we don't cry. You see, we both turned forty this month."

"No way," I said. "You ladies barely look thirty." They smiled as if to say they knew better.

"Do you want to look at the flash and get some ideas?" I asked. They said no, they already knew what they wanted. Barbara told me they were both scientists. She researched butterflies. Her friend, Maria, researched a parasite that lived on sharks. I never did get the parasite's name. They pulled out their books and showed me their pictures. They wanted me to draw, and I was happy to oblige them. I started drawing the butterfly with its four wings and its sharp middle section.

"Oh, you are doing a fine job," Barbara said. "Look at that detail. What an eye he has!" She smiled at Maria, then back to me. "This is why we chose you," she said.

"Why?"

"The name of your shop. The Painted Lady. It's a kind of butterfly."

"Really?"

Barbara spelled it on a napkin as she said it again. "Cynthia cardui: The Painted Lady."

Just the way she talked, I imagined that she was a good teacher.

"It's a powerful migrant, moving regularly throughout Northwest Europe from countries of overpopulation in North Africa. It has several caterpillar food plants, but it loves thistle best." She flipped a page and pointed to it. The butterfly had some brown, some orange, some yellow. She told me now how they flew during the day, not night.

"I can give you a beautiful tattoo," I said. I continued drawing, just the way I saw the butterfly in my mind. I didn't need to look much at her image on the page. Now it was in my mind. My hand went smooth over the page—up and down, back and forth, in long strokes and short ones.

"Oh, you are good," said Barbara.

"Yes," said Maria. "A fine artist."

No one had ever given me this much encouragement. My hands felt light and free. The women asked questions about how I got started and where I worked before this and if I had a girlfriend. I told them about Cheryl and her concerns that the shop couldn't make it.

"Oh, but you must never stop drawing," Maria exclaimed.

Within thirty minutes I had the outlines of their tattoos. I put them through the transposer and held them up for the ladies to examine.

"Beautiful," Barbara said.

"Perfect," said Maria.

"Okay, where?" I asked.

Maria wanted hers on her bicep, a real jock type. I had to explain how, in years to come, the skin would sag and the tattoo would look like a faded, stretched balloon. She and Barbara exchanged looks. She picked her ankle instead. Barbara chose to have her butterfly just below her collarbone.

"You two are sure? Once you've got it on, you've got it for the rest of your life."

"We're sure," they both said.

Barbara said she would go first. "Will it hurt?" she asked.

"It will hurt," I said. "But nothing you can't take."

In that moment, I thought of my mother. She had asked the same question about chemo. I showed Barbara the sterilized equipment, the surgical soap, caps to mix the colors, the latex gloves to cut the risk of infection and explained how I outlined first, then filled in the outline with color. In that moment, I felt proud and happy, but something more: I felt fulfilled. There have been times I just couldn't do my best work, too many other things to think about, like when I was taking my mother for chemo every week. We carried an aluminum bowl back and forth and my car smelled of vomit for months. But right now, in the city of Hartford, in my new studio, I was flying. These ladies submitted their bodies to me, and when someone puts her body right before you, with the legitimate fears of dirty needles and bad art, and still trusts you... well, you feel humbled by it all.

When I finished with Barbara, she stood up and examined herself in the mirror. She turned and looked at me in a way nobody has ever looked at me, like I was an artist. She gave me a kiss on the cheek. Then, Maria got into the chair, and I did her. She was quieter, but I watched the expression on her face as the parasite took shape. It was love. She loved that thing with a passion. Why else would you dedicate your life to something that looks like a leech? When I finished, she had tears in her eyes.

"Thank you, Willie," she said in a whisper.

Then Barbara took out her camera, and we started taking pictures. First, I took one of the two of them together, and then they each took one of me with the other.

"This is so much fun," they said. "You did an incredible job."

"I've got something, too." I smiled. "My own Painted Lady." Their eyebrows went up. "Do you want to see it?"

"Yeah," they said. "Show us."

I was feeling good on the talk of my talent. I wanted them to see my best work. I wanted to share my passion. Next thing, I dropped my pants to show the Painted Lady curled around my upper thigh. They giggled and covered their mouths, but as soon as they got used to me in my underwear, they came closer.

"Such vivid colors," Barbara said. "Like stained glass."

I pulled my pants up.

"You must make your girlfriend see that you are an artist," said Barbara.

"You must tell her that if you stop drawing, you will be tearing out your heart," Maria added.

I shook my head. "If you want to help me, send your friends here for tattoos."

The ladies promised they would, that I would have ten new clients that week, then they gave me their cards. I helped them collect their books and bags and off they went, through the door, the sun shining down on their freshly tattooed bodies.

After the ladies left, the shop was quiet again. I calculated that even if the ladies found me ten new clients and those ten found me ten more, sooner or later, the pyramid of referrals would taper off. And then, would it be enough? Maybe for me, but maybe not for Cheryl, because she could not see in me what I saw in myself. But the ladies had given me something more valuable than clients. They had seen my talent. The thought of it was exciting. A true professional, they had called me. I was just starting to reorganize my flash when the door opened again.

In walked that girl, the one Nemo had forced me to finish carving, the golden Hostess cupcake.

"You opened your own shop," she said.

"I did."

"How's business?"

"Fine," I said. I paced around the shop, swiping a dust rag over the furniture, then the windowsills as she looked through the flash. The street looked so quaint with its handsome signs hanging over every shop. So professional. Not like Nemo's operation at all.

"Can I get a tattoo?" she asked.

I didn't ask what she wanted, and I didn't wait to hear what might be coming next. "I don't think so," I said. "I didn't feel comfortable the first time, and I don't think I'm the right artist for you. Now, if you don't mind, I was just going to close up for today."

She zipped up her jacket and hoisted her bag over her shoulder. "There are a million of you guys," she said. "I thought I was doing you a favor."

I didn't respond. I just waited and locked the door behind her and pulled down the shades. I opened my sketchbook and started to draw. It was the Painted Lady taking shape, with more dimensions than I ever remembered. She was full of suffering, loss, love, and happiness, all rolled into one, caught by me, through my art. I got out a fresh piece of paper and started to draw.

CHOICES

Lois Green looked out the passenger window and admired her flowers as her husband pulled the car into the driveway. Every fall, she untangled the limbs of her climbing roses and laid them out on the ground as if she were preparing a body for burial. After she spread them out, she covered them with soil—soil she'd dug from the side of a grassy hill and transported by wheelbarrow, first breaking the clods of dirt with her fingers so she sprinkled it fine, just like flour on a pastry board. Then she layered mulch over that, smoothing the mound with the edge of the shovel. She always felt a knot of grief as she did this, one she carried with her until spring, when she could uncover the spindly limbs.

The sight of the vines each spring filled her with joy, and she loved to share clippings with friends and neighbors—this year, five to Ethel Loveridge, a few to Melvin King and his wife Gladys, and the sweet yellow shrub variety to Jon Ayers, the quiet school janitor who lived down the road. All told, Lois had cut her bushes down by half, but she admired them now as they tumbled over their trellis posts like seaweed swept along the ocean. She decided next spring she'd start a bed closer to the house, and she'd get some of those Grandifloras;

she loved the way they clustered, succulent as grapes. Just thinking about them made her mouth water.

Lois knew she should be thinking something else, something more connected to her husband and the doctor's news, rather than visualizing how the rose blossoms would bleed together like an impressionist painting, but as her husband, Green, pulled the car near the house, the only thing Lois wanted was to lie down near the trellis and inhale the perfumed fragrance until her body held it like a bottle.

The fact was that Green was dying. He had cancer, and it wouldn't be long before he was dead, a man who was crass and boisterous and big all his life, shrinking down in weight and voice and energy, everything dissipating the way a snow pile did when fierce winds swept over it. Soon she'd be alone with the child, in peace, in quiet. It's all she ever wanted—or at least she'd told herself this enough times to make it true.

As they sat silently in the car, ambivalence passed between them like the pulse of a magnetic field, each of them negative poles rejecting the other. The taunting, the meanness, the drinking had eroded, but a secret remained at the core of their marriage and, seeing the fear in his eyes now, she couldn't let him die without knowing. That's the least she could give him, now.

Patsy, the daughter, sat in the back seat and waited for some cue from her mother. The connection between them was as obvious as if they were one plant—the daughter flower, the mother stem. When Lois fidgeted, brushed her long hair off her neck, Patsy fidgeted too, flicking her ponytail from side to side. The older children rarely visited. They were much older than Patsy—with children near her age—and when they did come, their shadows crossed the threshold more boldly than they themselves dared.

"Well, you plan to sit in the car all day?" Green touched his wife's shoulder as he spoke.

"Nothing waiting in the house but dishes. Don't see any hurry for that."

Green shrugged, a half motion that left one shoulder hunched higher than the other. That vagueness Lois never associated with him. It scared her the same way strangers who appeared at the front door scared her.

"Come," Lois nudged him out of the car and led him by the sleeve across the yard toward the roses. "Go get a blanket," she yelled back to Patsy.

Patsy nodded and ran to the house.

Green walked slowly, feeling the ground beneath his feet. He stumbled over a mole hill and grabbed the rose post for support. It groaned beneath his weight.

"I should cut you some new ones," he said. "These are all rotted."

"What do I want new ones for?" Lois snapped. She didn't want Green thinking and talking about the future.... He never had before. They waited in silence as Patsy galloped toward them, a white blanket floating back from her shoulders like an angel's wings.

"Lay down," Lois ordered her husband once she'd spread the blanket beneath the canopy of roses. Green removed his shoes and sat on the edge of the blanket.

"Down," she pointed. After he lay back, so did she. There was just enough room for Patsy to lie on her other side. None of them spoke. They could hear the pigs knocking about in the barn—it was the kind of day that carried sound a great distance.

A rose petal dropped and floated down near Green's ear. Lois reached for it and saw that her husband's cheeks were wet. He put his arm over his eyes. She unfolded the arm and held it in her own. Its narrow length must belong to someone else, she thought as she caressed his dry skin, not the fat, gruff man she'd married. She reached for Patsy's hand. It lay limp, the girl was asleep.

"That kid could sleep through anything," Green marveled. He leaned on one elbow, his eyes still red, but dry now. His daughter's eyes fluttered under their lids. The downy hairs on her face shone gold in the sun. "She won't miss me," he said to Lois. "The other kids, maybe," he added. "And it's them who should hate me."

"None of them hate you," Lois said. "You know that."

Green twisted some roses off the vine and held them out to his wife. He'd given her flowers three times during their marriage, when the first three kids were born—but none at Patsy's birth.

Lois took the flowers and laid them on Patsy's chest. They lifted and receded like a tide, synchronized to Patsy's breathing.

"I always thought she'd be the one to go," Lois admitted. "I thought that would be my punishment. I was sure of it." The flowers spilled over and she arranged them again. Then, because she couldn't figure out exactly where to start, she just started talking.

Auction morning came, and it was a hard-weather day, cold and wet. The rain wouldn't let up at all. Puddles spotted the driveway; sheets of water hit the pig pen, running off the eaves, and then driven by the wind through the windows, mixing with the pigs' own bedding, forming muck they waded through.

Lois listened to the local polka station as she fried kielbasa and eggs for Green's breakfast. She turned from the stove to see him stomping across the yard, no hat, his jacket soaked, mud and blood caked on his arms.

"Get me a goddamned rag," he yelled as he stepped into the house.

She ran and fetched a bath towel.

"Not this." He threw the towel over her head. "That's a good towel. Can't you see my hands?" He waved them in her face.

Lois backed into the kitchen and returned with a clean dust rag.

"That son-of-a-bitchin' cow is sick," he said as he wiped his arms. "I'm going back to Maselli and I'm telling him, 'Give me my fuckin' money.' Then that's it. I never do business with him again. Second goddamned time in a month."

He went to the phone and dialed.

"Mrs. Fleming? Tell your old man I got a job for him this morning," Green said. "I got a cow needs dressing right away." He squeezed the phone to his ear as he listened. "An hour's okay. I can't wait. I've got to get some animals to auction, but Lois can tell him what we need."

"Get dressed," he said when he hung up the phone. "You've got to help me load these pigs and get them the hell out of here."

Lois wiped the mud from the phone and rinsed the sponge under the tap. "I said I'd raise them for you. But I can't put them in the truck. That's your job."

"You get your coat on right now," he snapped. "Don't give me any lip. I got to get them to the auction today, not next week."

"What difference does it make?" she asked. "One week."

"I just got stuck on a sick cow. We need that money this week." He grabbed her jacket off the hook in the entryway and held it in his fist, twitching in the open space between them.

She opened her mouth and immediately he shifted his weight, braced himself for a fight. She knew the pose. She took the coat without a word, jammed on her rubber boots, and stomped out the door.

He'd sworn to her that if she raised the pigs, he'd never make her help at auction time. She couldn't feed them, raise them from spastic piglets to their adult fullness, if she had to put them on that truck, ultimately bound for slaughter. At the auction, they would be sold and loaded for transport to the slaughterhouse in Pennsylvania. He'd promised her she would have no part in that. All those months they lined up at the door to greet her. They knew her. They trusted her.

"Don't make me do this," she yelled back to Green.

His face loomed through the storm. "Get yourself a bucket of feed. Go in the way you always do. I'll back the truck up, and you lead them in."

She could barely breathe. The force of the rain prevented the pigs from hearing her until she opened the door. Then they looked up from their huddle, ears flopped over, heads tilted. With small grunts they trotted over.

Was it her imagination? It seemed to her they didn't come as close as most days; they kept to one wall, watching. From outside, Green removed the door. Now the pigs crowded around her, flanked her, backed into the corner away from Green and the truck. They squealed with fright.

"Bring 'em this way," Green gestured. "Show 'em the grain." He disappeared into the bowels of the truck.

Lois lowered the bucket and shook it so the pigs could see and smell the fine grain. Their wet nostrils quivered. She shook the bucket again. "Don't come," she whispered. "Get back."

But they followed, fighting for a taste from the pail. When she stepped onto the platform Green had laid bridging the truck and the coop, the first pig hesitated, but the one behind pushed him and then they were all moving forward, into the truck.

Green slipped behind her and slammed the metal gate into place. The animals squealed with fright. At that moment, Lois' stomach contracted, and she almost screamed out, her reaction immediate, unconditioned.

The child should know nothing of auctions and slaughter. *Fetus*, she scolded herself. *Fetus. Fetus. Fee-tus.* There was not going to be a child. There was no child. Behind her, Green waited, brooding, angry.

"Get out." Green tugged on her sleeve. "Come on out of there now."

She allowed him to pull her back into the empty sty. "They know what's happening," she cried. "They know it." She squeezed her eyes shut against the image of the sharp blade, the blood purling first around the cut, then gaping like an evil grin of death.

Green waved her out the door. "I had to have help," he said. It was the closest thing to an apology she'd get. "I'll be back by four, five at the latest. Make sure Fleming grinds us enough hamburger. It'll stretch farther."

Lois nodded, yes, yes, anything to get rid of him. She pressed her hands on her abdomen. There would be no child. She had her future planned. In three years, Patsy would be eighteen. She'd get her freedom then.

Lois huddled against the side of the barn and smelled the moldy shingles. She could hear the pigs knocking against the sideboards as Green pulled the truck away. They squealed with distempered frenzy. She shivered and covered her ears. There would be no child.

The cold rain soaked her. She deserved it, she thought. They'd trusted her, and she'd led them to slaughter. She tried to sort the disconnected threads… smooth them out in her mind. First, the pregnancy. They'd been drunk. She'd ignored the queasiness until she couldn't ignore it any longer, then she'd made the appointment. Now she thought of the pigs moving along the line at the steel gray slaughter house, passed from hand to hand, first whole, then in pieces. Her stomach roiled, and she bent toward the ground. She had no idea how much time had passed when she heard Fleming's voice behind her.

"Excuse me, ma'am. Mrs. Green? You all right? Can I...?"

She pulled herself up straight before he could finish his question. "I didn't see you there," she said. "How long you been standing there?"

"Just got here," he lied. "Are you all right?" When Lois waved a hand to dismiss his concern, he asked, "Green around? He called about that cow?"

Jack Fleming was a handsome man. His plaid wool jacket showed beneath yellow rubber overalls that made washing the blood off easy. He had a wife and two kids. The butchering business had been his father's. He worked hard and was better off than most people in town. He and his wife were active Presbyterians. A contentment showed on his face. Lois liked him.

"He went to auction," she said, reaching for a shovel to begin cleaning manure from the pen. "He told your wife that."

"Oh." Fleming held the door as Lois stepped out of the rain. "That's doing the hard work," he observed as she began shoveling. "You ought to go to auction, leave this to Green."

"I hate those auctions." Lois leaned on the shovel. "They give me nightmares."

He waited for her to explain.

"They all know they're dying," she said. "You can tell by looking at them. I raise them, and it seems wrong to do both, raise them and kill them."

"I hear you," Fleming said. "I think about it, too." He pushed his cap back on his head as if to give himself more room to think. "You know the way the Indians handled it? Whatever they hunted—take the buffalo, let's say. They thanked them." The wonder of it settled on his face. "Yeah, they held a big ceremony, just to say thanks. Once they did that, they knew they were okay."

Another wave of nausea hit Lois. "I got to go eat some breakfast." She dropped the shovel and moved past him.

"I need you to tell me what you want," he said, following her out the door.

"Give me half an hour," Lois waved him back. "Then I'll be out."

After she was sick, she made Fleming some coffee. She kept the polka station on loud so she couldn't hear the gunshot that would signal the cow's death. When enough time had passed, she dressed and headed for the barn.

The barn smelled slightly metallic. Fresh blood scented the cold autumn air. Lois felt the bile rising up in her again and she took a few deep breaths. Fleming worked at the end of the long aisle; she could see his shadow cast by the bare bulb he'd hung high on the rafters. From a distance, the cow was a huge dark mass hanging in the air. As she moved closer, she saw the giant hooks through the tendons of the back feet. The cow's head pointed toward the ground and her carcass swung eerily to and fro, acknowledging defeat. A crimson stain spread like a web beneath her and trickled off to one corner.

Fleming faced the cow. Lois watched as he grasped his cutting knife and tore a line from the cow's hind quarters to her neck. Then he peeled back the skin, revealing a gelatinous pouch tucked in the cow's belly, and within that pouch, a Holstein calf the size of a puppy.

"*No!*" Lois reeled back and slid down the wall. "You— you killed it!"

Fleming jumped at the sound of her voice and the knife fell into the puddle of blood.

"Hey." He dipped his hands in a steamy bucket of water and wiped them clean. "Take it easy, now. You okay?" She shook her head.

"That little thing's been dead a while," he assured her. "Might be what made the cow sick." His voice took on a reflective tone. "No use getting upset. It just happens that way sometimes." He moved Lois back down the aisle and around the corner. "Let me walk you back to the house?"

Lois shook her head. She kept her eye on the barn door and when she reached it, she crossed the threshold quickly. "Just leave me here. I don't want that meat in our freezer, though. I don't care what you tell Green. You take it out of here."

Fleming studied her face, and then he nodded and turned away. Lois pulled shut the door. The rain had turned to a light snow and tiny flakes swirled around her. She tipped her face up, closed her eyes, and let the snow melt on her hot skin. When she opened her eyes, the snow had stopped. She never kept her clinic appointment.

"You would have done that?" Now Green hugged his arms to his body, as if opening them on the air, or near her, would endanger his own life. "You would have done it?"

She picked up one of the roses and pulled a silky petal, rubbing it like a coin between her fingers. "You do things you never expect. It seems impossible now—looking at her sleeping so peacefully—I probably would've turned right around and come home."

The sun beat fiercely on her head, and she could feel the sweat beading on her scalp, exposing the lie. "No," she said, "that's not true. I'm sure I would have done it. If I hadn't seen that cow, I would have."

Green slicked his hair back behind his ears. It grew thick and straight, as if it hadn't yet gotten word of the body's illness.

"You stuck to her like glue. You fed her off your breast. You didn't do that with the other kids. You sang to her, you never put her down. I can't believe you would have done it."

Lois shrugged. She knew she would have.

"She made me want to be with you," Green admitted. "I wanted to be her father. I didn't want anybody else to give you that. I thought she was someone else's. I figured for a long time you'd leave me. Fleming would come talk to you or some stranger would pull up for directions and I'd think, 'This is it, she's leaving now.' And the truth is, you didn't even want her."

Green sat with his legs folded, a pose Lois hadn't seen before. She didn't remember him ever sitting on the lawn. Ever. She checked the panic she felt watching him melt into the earth. The walls of her own resistance cracked just a little, and once the fissure began, a tide of emotion pressed against it and suddenly she was crying, full of grief and anger. She saw his weakness for the first time. After all those years of hate and resentment. Why did he have to wait so long to show her? Why show her at all?

Green rubbed her back, first tentatively, then with long, heated strokes. Lois wanted to fight it, scream, "Deal with it alone; I'm done with you," but the heat of his hand reached her muscles—they were sore and tight—and his touch felt good. The truth was, there were times, years at a time, when she had wished for his death. But now, she didn't want him to die. She wanted to take back all the hurtful things they'd done to each other; she wanted the hope of their future back. Lois bowed her head into the crook of Green's neck. His heart beat strongly. She listened to it and gazed at their child, still asleep, youth covering her face.

Unseen Angels

That morning, I intended between morning and afternoon chores to walk the boundaries of the farm, to see what fences needed to be mended before we could put the cows to pasture. But the night before, I had spent too much time and lost too much money at the casino, and as I reached the southernmost boundary of my old man's farm, I could not will my body back to chores, but only forward, toward the horizon. I passed the old dump, the housing project, and the baseball field where I spent the hours of my childhood that weren't delegated to work. And, then I kept going further still, past the old market that had since become a Chinese market to accommodate the needs of the Chinese immigrants working at the casinos for next to nothing and living like sardines in rickety houses along the city bus line. I kept going and going further still to the state road that ran to the casino, only I didn't go in that direction. I ran from it like a man being chased by demons. I crossed the highway and hitched a ride with the first trucker who stopped.

"Heading to New Jersey if you want to go that far," the trucker called across to where I stood on the road.

"Only to Windsor," I said, stepping closer. "Or as close as you go by there."

"No problem. Windsor, eh?" he asked.

I hopped up into the tall seat. I could hitch a ride there and back, and be back before afternoon chores. The cab was neat and tidy, smelled like apple tobacco and pine air freshener. The driver was a big fellow, over six feet. I could tell by the way his head grazed the roof above, with a build like a lumberjack. He stuck out his enormous hand.

"George." Medium brown hair was combed flat against his head and his face was square like the rest of him.

"Ryan," I said, taking his hand and giving it a quick shake.

"Did your car break down?" he asked.

I shook my head, but offered no further explanation of why I was hitching a ride to Windsor. But George glanced at me sideways. I could smell the manure on the cuffs of my jeans and the sweet smell of silage crusted around the hem as well. I could see he wanted to ask but, being someone who spent long hours alone, knew the importance of silence to a man who needed it. Still, when I saw how much he understood, it made me want to talk a little.

"You from these parts?" I asked.

George shook his head. "Louisiana, but I travel all over—east of the Mississippi mostly." He raised an eyebrow. "So what's in Windsor?"

"I want to go check out a monument. It used to be here, in Uncasville. But then the Indians made a fuss about it, and it got moved to Windsor."

"Monument of what?" George asked. He reached forward and turned the radio off. It wasn't playing too loud, but loud enough to hear the faint melody of Johnny Cash sharing hard times and cold truths. I was glad he turned it off.

"Monument to *whom*," I answered. "John Mason."

"Who?"

"One of the first English settlers to this area." I don't know why it made me feel better that he didn't know the name. But it did.

"It was a bloody time, wasn't it?" he said. "But still, not too different from now. Things don't change much, do they?"

"He was responsible for the slaughter of the Pequot Indians."

George flipped down his visor. "Those were different times," he said. "The way we thought about the Indians."

"That's why they moved his statue to Windsor. The Indians didn't think it was right to have him there on their sacred burial ground. But I don't know if removing history changes anything."

He was glancing in his side mirror, switching lanes but he was listening, and I appreciated that. No one had listened to me for a long time.

Before I knew it, he was leaning over to his glove compartment. He pulled out a bag of weed and some rolling papers.

"You smoke?" he asked.

"It's been a while," I said. It had been more than just a while. I was never much for drugs; I saw he kept a flask there as well, but he didn't offer it, and before he flipped the compartment shut I spied the pistol lying beside the flask.

"You remember how to roll?" he asked. So that was how I found myself rolling a joint and getting high early that cold April morning with George. I tried not to think about how much money I had lost the night before. I didn't let myself indulge too much because paranoia loomed at my shoulder, and I wanted to keep my wits—what few I had left—about me.

We listened to George's music selection. He had a souped-up stereo system. Willie Nelson's voice filled the cab.

"Precious memories, unseen angels. Sent from somewhere to my soul..."

"Willie Nelson? And that was Johnny Cash earlier. You like the old timers."

"Willie Nelson's the man," George said. "You know what he's done for farmers like you?"

"...sacred past unfold..."

I wasn't a farmer, though I came from a family of farmers in Connecticut. I wondered how George knew, but then I saw him staring at the cuff of my jeans. I had helped with chores just that morning because the farm hand hadn't shown up that day. My newspaper stories had been filed at the *Bulletin* the night before and I had the time free to help my old man milk, so I did. Now, I leaned my head against the window and closed my eyes, hoping George would just let the music be enough. I must have fallen asleep, because the next thing I knew we were parked facing a green square and the statue of John Mason straight ahead.

I expected to feel something—some connection—but looking at the bronze statue of John Mason, his sword tilted down to the earth, I thought how lonely he looked, this guy who was doing the thing that he had been commanded to do, that seemed like the honorable thing at the time. He led the slaughter of the Pequots and changed the course of American history, but history turned around so that the very sight of him was a scourge and an embarrassment.

I opened the truck door preparing to thank George, but to my surprise he opened his door too.

"Brought you this far," he said as though we had traveled half the country. "Might as well go with you to get a look at him, if you don't mind."

I said I didn't.

We crossed the street and made our way over to the green. I pulled out my phone.

"So why do you want to see this guy?" George asked.

I hesitated. "He's my ancestor."

"You want your picture taken with him?" George asked.

"No, thanks."

"Go on. You got nothing to be ashamed of." He pushed me in front of the statue, and I raised my hand over my brow to shield out the sun.

"You're not going to smile?" he asked.

"No."

He took the photo and made sure it was clear before handing my phone back to me. We heard some noise and looked up to see a few kids circling George's truck. The passenger door was open and one of the kids leaned into the glove compartment.

"Get away from my truck, you little bastards!" George yelled. One of them was holding the gun. "You drop it now, or I'll shoot you fuckers!"

The kid with the gun in his hand waved it in the air and released a shot.

Bang!

The teenagers laughed and scattered, leaving us with the echo of George's gun ringing out on Main Street as we ran to the truck.

"Get in," he shouted. "We have to get that gun."

A siren rang out in the distance.

"What? Are you crazy?" I was shaking my head, trying to understand, but I got in in the truck. "Let's report them and let the cops get it back. It's them who should be running. They were stealing from you."

"The gun's not registered," George said, popping the truck into second gear. "It ain't right, but the law's been keeping track of me." He winked. "Rather not get into it with the law." He reached under the seat and pulled up a semi-automatic.

"Holy fuckin' shit," I said. "Is that one registered?"

He gave me a crooked grin. "You're pretty funny. Now roll down your window."

I did, and suddenly I wondered if his truck might just be full of guns. I asked him, but he didn't answer. Instead he asked, "How's your aim?"

I hesitated, and he shrugged. "No matter, you don't need to be a sharpshooter to handle this." He tried handing me the semi. "We're going after them."

"How many guns have you got in this truck?" I asked.

"Have you heard of the second amendment?" he asked. "Your ancestors were fighting for our right to bear arms, weren't they?"

I was getting ready to educate him about the time frame of the Pequot War in the 1630s, more than a hundred fifty years before the Second Amendment, but the awareness of what he was really saying spread through my brain, like an oil spill, suffocating anything else. And, one of the kids had been dark skinned. I wasn't feeling good about where George was going with this.

"This is no different than your ancestor," he said. "Fighting for our rights. You got the legacy of that in your bloodline. And besides, they stole from me."

He gripped the wheel with one hand and the semi-automatic with the other. When he had restarted the truck, Willie Nelson had restarted too. George had to slow down just a bit to take the turn, and I opened the door and leapt from the truck, dropping into a ball on my side as I hit the sidewalk. There was a storefront, I didn't even know to what, but I scooted into the entry. I needn't have worried because George didn't stop, didn't even slow down. He sped up. That's when I saw the Confederate flag on his back bumper. Somehow, I had missed it when I had jumped into his truck. I slipped into the store—it was an appliance store—just as the police cruiser came around the corner, lights flashing. They were on to George, and I figured they'd get him before he got the teenagers, averting a tragic news story I would otherwise have to write.

I thought I'd steer clear of hitchhiking for a while, so I called a cab, and as I sat in the back seat, we circled back around to the green, where John Mason's statue looked out. I thought, then, maybe the natives had a point about removing symbols.

MERCIFUL LIKE
THE FATHER

The morning Mother Agnes came into River Star Ranch, I was putting flowers in vases on the tables—roses from my garden, something the customers appreciated. It was a little touch of beauty on this hot summer day just after they closed the tire burning plant. We knew the plant was in trouble before it closed because workers had been talking about it for weeks when they came in for the daily specials.

Earl and I had started offering fountain drinks and pie and a listening ear to people talking about how they were going to make a living. People here don't expect much out of life, but hard work is the one thing they do expect. I hoped the flowers would add some cheer. The plant had been the only real industry and had just spent seven million dollars in upgrades according to our first selectman, who sat around with the workers that morning, bemoaning the loss of the hundreds of thousands of dollars in real estate and property taxes and water fees.

"We'll have to make up that money in other tax rates now," Earl muttered.

His timing could have been better, and I told him so, which he didn't like but at least that shut him up.

I, myself, am not one for politics, but the discussion got political with the Republican folks cursing the liberals and their renewable clean energy policies; I kind of had to agree. Why did it seem that poor people were always the ones most hurt by "innovative changes?"

In fact, the town's per capita income had just inched above poverty level. This was not due to the tire burning plant, but to those who bought houses and land and commuted to Providence or Hartford for high paying jobs. We didn't see or like them much, but they kept the town from slipping back below the poverty line.

The story of the plant closing made the local paper, and Earl had just slapped it on the bar in front of me, knocking over one of the vases of roses as he did so, when Mother Agnes came through the door.

She was a beauty, albeit an aging one, and when I saw her, I was just plain jealous because looks don't last long in this part of the state; what poverty doesn't wear away, the rough environment does. She carried herself with a grace that someone might call regal, and she wore the nun garb but with a beret over her bonnet that only accented the peculiar bundle of her seeming contradictions. Her bonnet framed her striking face, the high cheekbones and luscious lips and peach colored skin. But it was her shimmery blue eyes that caught me.

She carried an armful of flyers with her.

"Good morning. Mind if I put up a flyer here?" she asked, approaching me.

"Maybe," I said. "I would need to take a look at it first."

She handed me the flyer. It gave a date one week from the present and the address of our local Catholic church, All Hallows, announcing a program called Merciful Like the Father. A Benedictine offering, it said, just below a picture of Mother Agnes and a man named Brother Zacharias.

"What is this program?" I asked.

"It's for the Jubilee year," she announced. I knew a little something about that, having been to church for the holidays when our priest had announced it. I had been Catholic most of my life, except for a few years when I had strayed away from the church. Jubilee years come along every twenty-five years with a big message attached; this time I was guessing had something to do with mercy.

She was saying something about having been assigned to our area as a mission and how lucky we were that our local church had been designated.

"For what?" asked Earl. He had never been religious and a person dressing up in religious garb meant nothing to him except a reason to be suspicious.

I think Mother Agnes knew she was in hostile territory at that moment, but she didn't let that stop her.

"To encourage growth from sin to grace, which every Christian is called to accomplish," Mother Agnes said.

The usual lunch crew was assembled, and they were listening but staying to the edges of the room in case they had to run.

I studied the flyer a little more.

"Why would you bring this flyer here, Mother?" Earl asked. "Are you familiar with this town at all? We just lost our only industry and people were already struggling."

The tire burning plant closing hurt our spirit even more than our pocket books because it seemed that no matter how hard people worked, they couldn't keep up with the changing times. The state and the federal government were both handing out contracts and dollars to companies creating energy from renewable resources, and our tire burning company, which kept about two hundred million tires out of landfills by burning and converting them to electricity couldn't make money in these changing times. But clearly,

Earl didn't believe Mother Agnes and her Jubilee program could help.

The first lunch customers started to fidget. Useless John, his second wife Erma, and young Willie Mann, who had needed John and Erma's emotional adoption of sorts after his mother died of breast cancer when he was seventeen.

"Holy years mark a time when our Lord pours forth his abundant graces. The bishop has heard and seen the needs of your community."

"What day is this program, Mother?" Willie chirped. He had an eye for pretty girls, and Mother Agnes' being a nun, and an older woman at that, didn't stop him at all.

"I'll come to your program," he said. "Abundant graces. Where do I sign?"

Erma, who couldn't hold a candle to Useless' first wife Becky, in my book, gained some points on this day, when she said, "Wait a minute, Willie. You're not even Catholic."

Mother Agnes handed Willie a flyer. "Makes no difference. Please, I hope you will join us. Bring your friends."

Willie squinted at the flyer more closely. "Where exactly is this?"

Mother Agnes was watching with great focus, like a bird of prey—at least, that was my opinion then.

"Hell, Willie," Useless said, jabbing Willie in the ribs. "I say go. You could use a little saving."

The regulars laughed good-naturedly.

The kitchen help came into the room then, carrying a tray of steaming water glasses fresh out of the dishwasher. Earl started lining them up on the buffet table.

"It's a beautiful part of the state you have," Mother Agnes said.

"Stick around, and we'll put you to work," Earl said. "Someone must have some hay to bale around here."

"I bale hay," Mother Agnes said. "And we milk goats and make cheese, too. I did my chores this morning before coming here."

Earl nodded. "You can leave those flyers, Sister, as long as your program is not for profit. We don't allow advertising for profit here."

I don't know if Mother Agnes was used to being dismissed like that. My husband has a heart the size of a blue whale's. His heart is that big, but surrounded by the prickliest shell. A person just never knows for certain how to approach Earl. I could have told Mother Agnes that if she showed up without her bonnet, hair down and a winning smile, Earl would be all ears. We've been married a long time, and I know his weaknesses, but I am proud to say he worked hard to overcome them in recent years.

"It's totally free," she said, shifting her weight from one well-shaped hip to the other. A little bead of sweat formed over her plump lip and despite myself, I thought how beauty had been wasted on this woman.

Mother Agnes handed me the flyers and went on her way. I got some tape and taped the flyer near the door. Willie pulled out his iPhone and started browsing the Internet.

"Holy shit!" he said. "Get this. Mother Agnes gave up being a Hollywood film star to become a nun."

"Well, what kind of nonsense is that?" Earl asked.

But I was intrigued. I sat down next to Willie, and he and I, heads bent together, read what we could of her story there on the Internet. She had starred with some of the greats—Elvis Presley and Warren Beattie, to name two.

"Wow!" Willie flashed a glossy photo of Mother Agnes as a teen, and everyone agreed she was stunning.

Willie went on reading, but more people were filtering in for lunch and the mood of the crowd was focused on the loss of the tire burning plant, not some Hollywood beauty.

True to her word, Mother Agnes returned to town the next week, and when she pulled her little Chevy into the All Hallows parking lot, she looked disappointed with the turnout. Aside from a group of sisters from a parish a few towns over, it was Willie and me. The church basement was a second home of sorts for Willie, since A.A. met there every week and Erma and John had gotten him to go. John was Willie's sponsor and John walked his talk, but he wasn't big on the institution of the church.

"I couldn't convince them," Willie shrugged. "I just think she's an interesting character," he said. "Don't you? Who would give up a promising career in Hollywood to become a nun? There was a documentary about her, which I watched too. I don't think she's an ordinary person." This last observation he whispered as Mother Agnes swished by us to welcome the man we recognized from the flyer as Brother Zacharias. He apologized for being late for the set up, which our local nuns had already done, placing chairs in a half circle and two urns, one of coffee and one of hot water, on a card table with cream and sugar.

And Mother Agnes did not disappoint Willie. She started telling stories from the New Testament, the same old stories I had heard all my life, but this time I was hearing them from a different slant. Mercy? It was a word I knew but not an idea I understood until I heard it from Mother Agnes. She was telling the story of Peter weeping after his betrayal of our Lord, but instead of emphasizing Peter's denial of Christ, she was talking about forgiveness and how God manifests his power by forgiveness. I had lived long enough that forgiveness held interest for me, but I couldn't see how Willie at his age would grasp onto the subject. He had his sketchpad out, and as Mother Agnes was speaking, he was sketching. I wondered if we'd see some variation of Mother Agnes as a tattoo offering at his shop and I made a note to caution him about this later.

And maybe it all would have gone fine if it had ended there, but it didn't. We heard the door open upstairs and footsteps as people descended into the basement, the elder Mrs. Leminsky leading the way. Theirs was an old Polish family with roots back several generations in town. The grandmother was a faithful Catholic. But when I saw her daughter-in-law, whose name escaped me, and granddaughter, Anna, I knew there would be trouble.

They scraped their folding chairs along the floor as they settled into them and set their eyes, not upon Mother Agnes, but straight upon Brother Zacharias. He nodded and smiled a greeting and asked if we all knew each other, which of course, we did in some way.

He repeated Mother Agnes' last point about the Jubilee year and the theme of mercy and how mercy was compassion to be shown for those who had no claim to receive kindness.

"Like you gave Reggie Rawlins?" snapped Anna. Her sister Tracy had been one of Reggie's victims. Anna was a fine girl and the weight upon her shoulders had been too heavy since her sister had died. Anna had been pregnant at the time and, when her little girl was born, she named her Tracy.

Brother Zacharias cocked his head.

"Do you know who we are, Brother Zacharias?" Mrs. Leminsky asked.

Brother Zacharias shook his head. He looked at Mother Agnes, and she shrugged, and then he said, "I'm sorry, I don't. Please, tell me."

When Tracy's grandmother said "Leminsky," Brother Zacharias' face flushed. His features, which had been bright, darkened and creases folded across his forehead and along his mouth.

Willie and I looked at each other. Of course we knew the Leminsky family's tragedy, but how was it that Brother Zacharias knew it with them just saying their name? He had traveled from a Benedictine monastery from the far west corner of the state, which was really a world away from Asheville—or so we thought.

"We came to see how this mercy works. How could you be spiritual advisor to a serial killer and give burial to the animal who savaged our girl, and not only her, but also seven others? He raped and sodomized them and tossed them into the woods, and you take and give him a Christian funeral and burial?"

Contrary to taking their attack as such, Brother Zacharias pulled his folding chair closer into the circle and leaned forward.

"First, I want to say I am so sorry for your loss." He looked at each of them and held their gaze, but his words rang hollow. Still, there was no denying the power of their loss and Anna was the first to break into tears, and then her mother. But Mrs. Leminsky, the matriarch of the family, held fast.

"You gave that animal a Christian burial. After what he did, how could you do that?"

Brother Zacharias folded the Bible he had in his hands and slid it under his seat. "He confessed Jesus as Lord, and it was and is my responsibility as a servant of Christ to offer him God's mercy."

I could see Willie was not expecting this either, and he and I were both working to make the connections that were already clear to Brother Zacharias and the Leminsky family. But Mother Agnes looked totally confused, and it was Willie who spoke.

"You probably know the story of Reggie Rawlins, Mother?"

"He was the last person who died in Connecticut on death row before the state made the death penalty illegal," she whispered.

"Thank God they got him first," Anna's mother snapped. These were the only words she spoke the entire time in that basement.

"He chose to die to save the families any more pain and suffering," Brother Zacharias corrected her.

"Save us pain and suffering!" Mrs. Leminsky uttered.

"And believe me, he found very little peace even after his conversion. The depth of horror about his own deeds haunted him. They were truly horrible deeds." Brother Zacharias shook his head, his eyes pleading to the Leminsky women.

Mother Agnes opened her hands out to them. "How can we help you?" she asked.

Mrs. Leminsky analyzed Mother Agnes' face, a face that burned with beauty, but more importantly perhaps to Mrs. Leminsky, sincerity.

"Not a day goes by, Mother, without some picture of what he did flashing through my mind. I can't erase it. And we certainly can't forgive it."

Mother Agnes swallowed. She looked at Brother Zacharias and frowned. "Before we set out here as a team, we should have given this more careful consideration. What happened in this corner of the state was a horror." She shook her head. "I didn't know all of… this."

Brother Zacharias' jaw clenched. "It is our job to show compassion—the compassion of Jesus—to everyone, Mother."

"No doubt," Mother Agnes said, standing and smoothing her robe. "No doubt about that. But I would like to show consideration for the depth of the wound here, Brother Zacharias, and I would like to do that now. I think if you would be so good as to see this wound as clearly as you saw the wound in Reggie Rawlins. These women need something more from us right now."

Brother Zacharias looked at the three Leminsky women. "What?" he asked. "What is it you want from me?"

"We want your apology, Brother Zacharias."

He swallowed. "I am sorry for your pain."

"No," Mrs. Leminsky said. "Not that—for burying that animal with a Christian burial."

"I can't," he whispered. "That, I cannot do."

Mother Agnes stepped between Brother Zacharias and the Leminsky women.

"Allow me to pray with you," she said. "Brother Zacharias, this program is done for today, and I ask you to let me minister to these women."

Brother Zacharias got up from his chair, tucked his Bible under his arm and faced the Leminsky women one last time. "I am sorry for your pain." And then he left the room. Mother Agnes turned to the three nuns who had come from a neighboring parish.

"If you, sisters, will be good enough to go into the kitchen and take the cold cuts to your nearest shelter, I would very much appreciate that. I will be in touch in a day or so." She waited for the women to leave the room. Willie and I looked at each other, preparing to be dismissed.

Mother Agnes addressed us next. "You are both locals, yes?"

Willie and I nodded.

"I invite you, then, to stay. It seems this wound affected the whole area, so many people. May we close this circle up?" And she dragged her chair next to Mrs. Leminsky.

"Will you allow me the honor of praying together, Mrs. Leminsky?"

Mrs. Leminsky nodded, and Mother Agnes took her hand. She bowed her head and closed her eyes, and we all did the same.

"Lord Jesus, it is often through a wounded heart that you come to us and we to you. Here, the hearts of these people and this community have been wounded. Come to us with your love and mercy. Show us, Lord, thy merciful face."

There was a long silence, and then Mother Agnes looked at Mrs. Leminsky and said, "I know you are a praying woman. Can you ask the Lord to show you His merciful face?"

Mrs. Leminsky squeezed her eyes shut and drew in a deep breath. When she opened them, she stared up at the stained glass windows, where the Stations of the Cross were painted.

"Can you tell me, Mother, what that looks like?"

If we had been expecting a bunch of fancy words that didn't ring true to our experience, we were wrong. Mother Agnes' eyes narrowed, and her gaze slid from Mrs. Leminsky to her granddaughter, Anna, and back again. "Perhaps the way you look at your granddaughter?" But her reply sounded more like a question, and she shook her head in frustration.

It seemed then the Leminsky women breathed a collective sigh of relief. Silence. Just silence. We could hear the toilet running in the other room and the sisters' little car engine backing out of the church parking lot. We could practically hear the things we didn't want to hear.

Then Mrs. Leminsky stood up and she said, "We didn't expect any answers, Mother. But we wanted to be heard. Thank you for hearing us."

Mother Agnes pressed a hand to her heart. "I heard you. And I am so, so sorry."

Mrs. Leminsky searched Mother Agnes' face. Was she saying she was sorry that Reggie Rawlins had gotten a Christian burial? Whatever she was saying, her sorrow was clear, and that seemed to be enough for the Leminsky women. They turned and went up the stairs, leaving Mother Agnes, Willie, and I standing in the basement.

Mother Agnes seemed to weave out of balance and sat back down in her chair. Willie went to get her a cup of water from the kitchen and, while he was gone, Mother Agnes said, "The arrogance of the Church continues to astound me. We don't have all the answers, and truthfully, I myself would like some." She looked up at me. "Can you take me to the place the Leminsky girl was found?"

"I am not sure exactly," I said. "But I know the general area."

We stopped talking when Willie came back into the room, and I understood she did not want to have him along, perhaps to avoid spectacle.

She accepted the water from Willie and thanked him. "You are a wonderful young man," she smiled. "Many blessings to you, young William."

Willie beamed as if the Pope had blessed him. "I think you really heard the call, Mother. I can tell just looking at you. Thank you."

And at that, he turned and went up the stairs, and we followed not too far behind and got into my Jeep.

I was aware of the ground-in mud on the mats and coffee stains on the leather. But I needn't have worried because Mother Agnes' attention seemed to be somewhere else, a long way off.

"So many people come to us with their suffering," she said. "So much suffering." She folded her hands in her lap. "Sometimes I don't know what to do with it all," she said.

She adjusted her beret on her head and then, on second thought, removed it.

"Are you sure you want to go to the site, Mother? You don't need to."

"People don't trust outsiders," she said. "But Reggie Rawlins was an insider."

"People just don't trust that much, in my experience, Mother."

"I can see why," she said. "Yes, please. I do want to go."

I drove away from the center of town out to the woodland. I wished the Leminskys and all the people could see what I was seeing, the suffering of Mother Agnes right now—not her own suffering, but her suffering on our behalf.

"This is beautiful," she murmured. We were traveling down my favorite road in Asheville, River Road, where the Quanduck River ran below, splashing up over the rocks and catching water in prisms of light. Little rainbows shimmered everywhere.

"Can we stop?" she asked.

I pulled over onto the bridge. A long, chewed-up road ran up the hill from there, the only way to reach old Mr. Howe's place. He'd been dead many years, but in Asheville, the places and the memories of the dead stayed way past their own lives. And on the opposite side of River Road, an underground spring fed a large pond, which seemed still on the surface. But, beneath the bridge, the river roared.

We'd had a wet summer, and the river swelled its banks and surged downstream. Mother Agnes leaned on the metal rail, and then she stepped off the bridge and onto the rocks.

"Stay right there, Mother," I said. "I want to take your picture." I went back to the car and got my phone and raced back across the bridge, descending toward her. The sun slanted out of the west, and I was trying to get it behind me when my foot slipped out from under me.

"Watch yourself, Marilyn! These rocks are slippery." Mother Agnes put her body in front of me to break my fall, but in doing so, she had nothing to hold onto and her feet came right out from under her and she slid on her side, black habit first hitching up to catch on a rock, but tearing as she shot into the water. The current was strong, and she went under. I lost sight of her, and then she bobbed up and started downstream.

"Help, Marilyn!" She went under again.

Already I was dialing 911. I thought I'd get in the river and pluck her out, but just in case, I made the call. No sooner did I get off the call, running along the bank where the river ran straight, and I thought she'd just stand up and hurl herself to shore. I expected that. Arms flailing, she grabbed a broken branch and it let go from the bank as she plunged further down the river, further from me. I started to think about all the kids we'd lost over the years to this river when it got engorged and spit them over the falls in Moosup.

"Mother, keep your head up!" I yelled. My voice carried into the roar of the current. I saw her face, her eyes filled with fear, then she looked up through the trees and the sunlight caught her face one last time before the current sucked her under and around the bend.

I scrambled up the steep bank, the wild branches ripping my skin and clothes. And I jumped in the Jeep, unaware how I got it turned around and onto the road. I sped back to town, dialing Earl.

"Mother Agnes is coming down the river," I shouted into the phone, hoping he heard before the cell signal cut out. Wherever I could take my eyes off the road, I peered to the river, looking for her. But the current moved fast, and the river was far below and the road too narrow. At the end of River Road, I turned left, thinking about where the river went and how to stay close to her. I thought if I could keep yelling, keep her yelling so she would know I was there, somehow we'd be okay. I couldn't think otherwise. She had gone into the river trying to save me from doing so.

"Please, God," I whispered and the only prayer I could think to say was the table blessing— "Bless us, Lord, for these thine gifts...." All the daily masses I'd attended—why that prayer? The mind does crazy things. I could hear the sirens now going off, the town officials getting their emergency vehicles mobilized, so I knew Earl had heard me.

"Hold on, Mother!"

As I sped through town, past the empty tire burning plant, people who lived in the old mill houses along the river came out of their homes and off their porches to stand in the street. The senior citizens, hearing the sirens, came out of the senior center. Both the center and the playground next to it had been donated by the plant, which stood empty on the hill above us. People snapped limbs off trees and ran to the riverbank. I parked along the side of the road and ran to join them.

Mother Agnes came bobbing and floating, like a rag doll into view, dead or unconscious we couldn't tell.

There on the bank stood Willie—he was a strong swimmer—shedding his tee shirt. He had no fear of death since his mother died, and he jumped in and grabbed her, the current carrying both of them now. We could see the gash on her head and the blood covering her face—a face tipped down, so her chin tilted to her chest. Thick blond hair plastered with leaves and twigs but her black habit still on her.

They bobbed along with the river sweeping them nearer to River Star Ranch, where Earl and Useless John waited. Willie tried to cut through the current to get closer to the bank. Earl and Useless John didn't wait; they jumped in and grabbed them, and it took all their strength to pull Willie and Mother Agnes free. There were others—too many to name—racing right to the edge of the bank, dangerously close to slipping in, but with no mind for threat or danger. A stretcher came down the slope, too, and then they were rolling Mother Agnes onto the bank and Useless, our senior EMT, was performing CPR. The ambulance lights flashed on the top of the bank, but I could already read Willie's face as he lifted her robe and wiped the blood from her face and her hair from her eyes.... The EMT stopped and they scrambled up the bank with Mother Agnes on the stretcher to get her in the ambulance to the defibrillator.

As she came up the slope on the stretcher, I fell into the line of people. We lined up like we were receiving our Lord himself. For now, Mother Agnes' face released from her bonnet, from all our pain and suffering, was the most beautiful face any of us had ever seen.

ACKNOWLEDGMENTS

Thanks to many for the love and perspective that have supported me to write. First, my family: parents Margaurite Hogan and Andrew Davis, Sr.; sister Jo-Ellen Converse and brother Brad Davis. Peter Kochenburger helped set me on my path and is a fantastic father to our sons. Fellow writers from a past writing group gave feedback on early versions of several stories: Wally Lamb, Susan Campbell, Doug Anderson, and Leslie Johnson. Melissa Rosatti and Sheila and Gerry Levine give wise counsel and help me see what's possible. Caroline Leavitt, brilliant writer and editor and one of the most generous human beings I know, offers me critique, advice, and endless moral support. Sandi Shelton, whose love and sparkly soul shines through all her work, has given years of incredible friendship, writing support, and meaning beyond words. Pam Browning, Jane Moynihan, Carol Konieczny and Katie Irish, friends for life, laugh and cry with me and have been heroes in times of need. Kim Burwick shows me friendship that knows no bounds of time or distance. Maria Decsy shares her spiritual wisdom as deep as the ocean. To the world's best agent, Rena Rossner, whose message and example, Never give up, breathes life into writers' dreams, and to Alex Slater for bringing us together. To the crew at Cornerstone Press for giving this book life. Your enthusiasm has been a great joy.

Most especially, I thank my trio of men: my sons, Ben and Alex Kochenburger, who inspire me every day and who never wavered in their belief; and Rui Varandas, for love and light, and sailing adventures that have shown me beauty in the world once again.

Gratitude goes out to the following publications in which these stories originally appeared:

"The Appointed Hour" (2016) and "The Law of Gravity" (2000) first published in the *Notre Dame Review*.

"The Object of Desire" (2005) first published in *Carve*.

"Dancing at the Sky Top with Andrea" (1998) first published in the *Hartford Advocate*.

"Destiny's Clothes" (2015) first published in *4ink7*.

"Useless John," originally published in *Vermont Literary Review* Summer/Fall 2002. Reprinted by permission of the publisher.

"John Mason's Eye" (1998) and "The Ancestor's Voice" (2002) first published in *descant*.

"The Painted Lady" (2003) first published in *Zone 3*.

"Choices" (1997) first published in *American Short Fiction*.

"Unseen Angels" (2016) first published in *Schuylkill Valley Journal*.

Cornerstone Press Staff

Dr. Ross K. Tangedal

James R. Agee

Caleb J. Baeten

Dakotah Bork

Cameron P. Crahen

Clara R. Davisson

Leah K. Dix

Caitlin N. Fischer

Nathaniel J. Hawlish

Mallory M. Jones

Jacob Kocken

Travis Loepfe

Ryan L. Loos

Merita Mehmedi

Alexis Neeley

Felycia M. Noblet

Tanner Olson

Isabella Pietsch

Lauren M. Santos

Samantha J. Smith

Natalie Wanasek

Amy K. Wasleske

Avonelle R. Weist

Hannah Wiedmeyer

Richard W. Wilkosz

Kathryn Wisniewski

About the Author

Susanne Davis is an award-winning writer. Her fiction and non-fiction have been included in the *Notre Dame Review*, *American Short Fiction, Harvard Law Bulletin, Feminist Studies, St. Petersburg Review*, and numerous others. She lives in Connecticut and teaches at Trinity College and the University of Connecticut. More information on Susanne Davis can be found on her website, www.susannedavis.com, as well as Facebook.com/Susanne.davis.336.